# FORGING A NEW AMERICA

# FORGING A NEW AMERICA

## How American Liberalism and Climate Change Landed Us in Siberia

### ROGER COLLEY

Liberty Hill Publishing

Liberty Hill Publishing
2301 Lucien Way #415
Maitland, FL 32751
407.339.4217
www.libertyhillpublishing.com

Paperback ISBN-13: 978-1-6628-2997-0
Dust Jacket ISBN-13: 978-1-6628-2998-7
Ebook ISBN-13: 978-1-6628-2999-4

# AUTHOR'S NOTE

⎯⎯⎯⎯⎯⎯ ★ ⎯⎯⎯⎯⎯⎯

On this day of January 21, 2021, we learned of our beloved son Lex's passing. His untimely, unexpected death ends the beginning of this novel, for Lex's life embodied the American dream. The dream my dad from Italy lived, assimilating into our American culture, learning the language perfectly, working hard, taking care of family, and succeeding on the merits.

Lex was industrious, independent, dedicated, competitive in business, cooperative with teammates, colleagues, and family, and most importantly kind. Everybody Loved Lex. By example, he lived the American dream! Work hard, achieve, succeed.

There is no reason for me to go on with this now, beyond its brief few pages written. I might not live the 12 years to my 95th birthday anyway. I will just hope and pray America will lead the way in human progress while retaining the values of the past that we know work so well.

**Roger Colley**

**ADDENDUM:** Two weeks later. My wife Janice and three of my good friends read the introduction, really liked it, and encouraged me to go on. My very smart college educated grandson, Rico Colley, thought the intro was 'brilliant" and that I should continue. And he is on the side of Alyssa no less. So, I continue, to keep it a short story novel, interesting, with a message, and dedicated to our beloved son Lex.

# TABLE OF CONTENTS

★

# INTRODUCTION

★

## NEW AMERICA

## 2033

The bright morning sunlight reflected brilliantly across the calm waters of the large bay all the way to our neighboring city across our divide. Lucky for us, it has been a very friendly divide. Sure, they speak Russian while we speak English, but we have been getting along quite fine these last ten years since I, and most of my family, arrived. In mid-winter February, it is quite cold out, but no snow and at least five degrees warmer than it used to be. That global warming stuff – seems we are in a gradual warming trend, part due to human activity, part due to the natural warming and cooling cycles of our planet, and part due to the increased solar explosion activity of our sun. The top climate scientists are still researching the combination, but the really smart guys are not convinced it's ninety percent due to our carbon dioxide emissions.

Waiting patiently for my great grandson, Alex, to arrive, I'll just have another cup of this fine Columbian coffee. No classes on Saturdays, but he always tends to come beyond his promised time. I don't quiz him, but I'm guessing he stays up late on Friday evenings having a good time after a grueling week of studies and sports. Yet, he is the one who persists in me telling him the story of how we got here, and in his trying to understand why his cousin Tyler is still back in what we call "Old America." Approaching my 95th birthday in another week, I sometimes have a difficult time remembering all the details myself. But anyway, I am sure glad I am here with most of my family. There are some twenty million of us here now in our new country with a million more coming every year. Legal immigrants we call them, and once their application is approved, we welcome them with open arms. I have to repeat to Alex that arrivals are all wedded to the ideals of freedom, justice, equality under the law, free enterprise, equal opportunity, and that they see the benefits of hard work, limited government, family, charity, and individual responsibility. We'll talk about all that later.

I love to muse and talk to myself when I'm home alone. Darling wife is out shopping already, and I can't get out on our nearby new golf course until April. So, I'm thinking that I'm just so thankful back in 2021 one of the richest Americans had the foresight to know what was happening to his beloved America. Unbelievable that he could negotiate this deal with the Russian oligarchs – a renewable ninety-nine year lease for some 60,000 square miles of land here opposite Vladivostok, the far eastern Russian city some eight days, 5500 miles by train, the Trans-Siberian Railroad, to Moscow. Picture a nice piece of land something like an inverted rectangle New York City to North Carolina some 400 miles, balanced by Atlantic City to past Harrisburg, some 150 miles, but millions of trees on hills and in valleys and before we came only occupied by about 450,000 people. And we also have the Frontier Territory, the 120,000 sq. miles of Siberian land some 1300 miles northwest of here just above the Russian city of Chita along the TS railway, not too far from the largest volume of water lake in the world, Lake Baikal, smack in the middle of Siberia.

So, sounds like we Yankees are far away, but as we find ourselves between Mongolia on one side of us and the Sea of Japan on the other, we are happy, and it's just fabulous that the dozen small Russian towns in our New America all voted overwhelmingly in favor of accepting the deal. After all, the deal is predicated on our paying the local Russians within our New America Central substantial sums for local improvements and better education for all. And yes, we do have universal healthcare, even for our Russian neighbors in our district, but of course not managed by our government, and we take very good care of those who suddenly cannot care for themselves. And so brilliant, our multi-billionaire founding father has the Russian oligarchs so very pleased with the Frontier part of the deal. We bring our best mining technology into the vast melting Siberian permafrost, bring out that valuable treasure of minerals, including the rare metals used in the high technology businesses, and pay the central Russian government very handsome royalties. The Russians love a little global warming! And our mutual defense pact even allows us to have a defensive military force including defensive missiles and a modern Air Force.

Hey! Finally, here he is. Medium height and build, Alex is a handsome kid, well not a kid anymore, twenty years old. "Okay, my boy, you made it. Have a good week?"

"Sure did, Papa Bear. Plenty busy, but hey, brought us some warmed up raisin bagels. Do we have more coffee?"

As I pointed him towards the kitchen of our nicely appointed condo where my darling wife of nearly seventy years of marriage had left another brewing pot, I glanced again out the floor to ceiling six-foot-wide glass patio door towards Vladivostok, the now modern Russian city to our southwest. I remembered the story that the city began as a small Russian military outpost some 400 years ago. The Russian negotiators back at that time convinced China to sign deals for Russia to go all the way to the sea as they expanded their control of the vast land area east of Moscow. They wanted to make sure the invading armies of the Mongolian Empire were kept away. I seem to recall some saying the land mass of Russia is larger than the whole continent of Africa. I'll ask Alex to check that.

"Okay, Papa Bear, let's talk. What today? You pick the subject. What's going on over there in that country you use to love so much?" Alex sat down in a comfortable chair next to his ancient great grandfather and set the two coffees and baked goods down on a within reach cocktail table. His eyes were bright, his intellectual curiosity unmistakable. Maybe it was his deep respect for his believing in the wisdom of someone who has been around a bit. I became the wise old sage.

"So, let's go," I replied in a firm, confident voice. "I'm going to continue the stories of your cousin Tyler, who wants to come here, and the love of his life, Alyssa, who is of the opposite thinking. You know, my boy, it's this unending conflict, the delicate ongoing part of our human nature. But, what's more in this natural ongoing conflict is my hope that out of intelligent, reasoning, opposing arguments, the near truth comes out."

# PART I

★

## THE U.S.A.

**2021 TO NOW 2033**

# CHAPTER 1

★

## ONE PARTY RULE

As usual, Tyler looked perturbed on these occasions. Only twenty years old and normally full of energy with his male friends, he nonetheless dreaded what was ahead. She would be here any moment. He was alone at home, a small apartment in Philadelphia just off campus. Yes, his parents had gone to New America two years prior. They had begged him to go with them. His thoughts were leaning towards their side, but at eighteen years of age he had convinced them he was legally independent, and that he would join them after his college graduation from the University of Pennsylvania. He swore to them that if he decided to join them, he would bring the love of his life with him too, if only he could convince her.

Tyler thought back to his freshman year, just twelve months ago, when he wasn't exactly sure where he stood politically. His father, grandfather and great grandfather surely were deeply disturbed where their America was heading and all herded their families off, far away to this New America place. They called themselves strong conservatives. His mom was all in favor of their concepts but also so empathetic towards those less fortunate. He remembered her pleading with them that the minorities, the handicapped, and the poorer working families all had to be taken care of. He couldn't remember how she voted. All he knew was that he had to find the answers himself.

He had an open mind, until that is he engulfed himself in finding out what was really going on out there, not what the professors and the press were feeding him.

Alyssa was also twenty years of age and now also a sophomore at Penn. They had met early in their freshmen year at a campus social function. A very pretty blond, clear skin, vibrant blue eyes, attractive figure, soft voice, high IQ. Little wonder that Tyler was so deeply in love with her. She fully returned his affections, but his problem was that she had fully accepted her parent's and her closest friends' and her university's positions on a vast array of social and political positions – but so problematic to him, for now a year later they seemed more and more the opposite of his. If only he could eventually persuade her it was not going to work, it meaning the new government system.

He would marry her in front of her parents and friends and then whisk her with him to New America where it was all working. His whole study of history in his freshman year was that past events were all so complex and often confusing, but if one could just sort out "what works and what doesn't work," then one could get through all the pure, diverse ideologies and come up with 'what's the best for the most.' And while he had not seen his wise old great grandfather known as "Papa Bear" since his 10th birthday, their frequent correspondence was on the same wavelength. More and more lately, he was beginning to look forward to getting to New America.

A short two knock on the unlocked door and in she came, smiling and exuberant. "Hi!" Alyssa rang out.

"Hey," Tyler said softly. "Good day in class? Sit."

"Yeah, political science. I love it. Prof admits it's not going well but it's going to turn around soon." She leaned over and kissed him on his cheek as Tyler never got up from the two-seat sofa.

"No ... no. It's not going to get better, only even worse," he retorted. "I've been studying this. One party rule becomes corrupt, and you learned didn't you that 'power corrupts, and absolute power corrupts absolutely."

"Yeah, yeah Ty, so said Lord Acton two hundred years ago. What did he know?"

"He knew from experience and observation – the truth... Listen, when the Democrats with their presidency won back from the conservatives and held the two bodies of Congress, they loaded the Supreme Court from nine justices to fifteen, they got statehoods for D.C and Puerto Rico with their Democratic Party free spending promises for racial minorities leading to big majorities in the House and Senate, exercising power under the welfare clause of our federal Constitution – their complete control, their one party dominance, it has only lead to over spending, huge federal deficits even with their higher taxes on the rich, wasted money on projects not working, incompetent government takeover of industries like healthcare, utilities, and autos..."

"Ty, Ty, stop!" Alyssa interjected. "You're all wound up. I just got here. All this change takes time to work out. Yes, the progressives are in charge. Your so-called 'radical left' has won out. The traditional Democratic Party is no longer what it was twenty years ago – lifelong Democrats are now beholder to the so called progressive left. But you have to give it time. It's all so new. We'll work out the bugs."

"Time to work out!" Tyler replied raising his voice. "Are you kidding? The Chinese control us now. This massive debt we're incurring has been financed by their buying our Treasury bonds and bills. Like my dad says, 'They own us." We don't manufacture anything here anymore. I've checked all this out. We have massive unemployment compensation, massive retirement payments, massive healthcare payments, massive educational payouts – where in the world do you think that money is coming from? Free education – the school buildings have to be maintained, the teachers have to be paid. Free healthcare – the nurses, the doctors, the hospitals all have to be paid. Debt financing just can't keep up with the needs of quality, so what happens? We end up with less and less quality of education, of healthcare." Yes, he was really wound up.

"Today there are so many, so many courses available in schools at all levels, why? In order to please everybody is the answer. No need is left unanswered. But the result is there are not enough trained, competent teachers available to solve every whim of the progressive, just as in medicine, not enough trained, quality nurses and doctors to solve every malady that befalls mankind. Targeting the fulfillment of perfection in imperfect human beings is impossible Alyssa."

She joined the fray raising her voice. "No. It's not," she countered. "We all wanted equality, and now we have equality for all of us. And we also have 'equity.' Equal results, equal outcomes. No more racial discrimination. Equity – no more 'have nots.' Five hundred years of white supremacy is over, Ty. If we citizens can't do it ourselves, then what's wrong with a benevolent government with noble leaders doing it for us?"

"Because it doesn't work. While it sounds nice, it is not in the cards that it can work. Big government becomes incompetent in execution. Leaders with bold intentions become self-serving. Why? Why, because my dearest friend, equality can only work in justice under the law, equality of opportunity not equality of outcomes. Because we humans are each different. We have a difference in the number of our brain cells, difference in our neurotransmitters, difference in our hormones, differences from experiences in our mother's womb, from our childhood experiences, from the influences of many, many environmental impacts-each of us is unique. Each of us react first to our five senses before the thinking part of our brains come into play. You cannot have an all knowing, benevolent government running the show for everyone because the leaders of that government and its vast bureaucracy simply are a group of different minded individuals who in the final analysis are each not thinking and acting alike.

"And in that final analysis most people tend to behave primarily to their own personal advantage, most become selfish, and that means potentially leading to personal corruption... The history of mankind is on my side. The corruption of our political leaders is already very obvious. It's already happening."

"You're wrong," Alyssa responded, regaining her position after absorbing his outburst. "You sound so smart, but you're wrong Tyler. And where in the world did you get all this so called knowledge you're mumbling about? Geez, a few months ago you never spoke like this. Is it your family in Siberia feeding you this garbage? As a nation, we have advanced far beyond what you have described. I will have my professor tomorrow in Political Science class refute your claims." The two turned away from each other's harsh stares at one another. The evening had not gone well.

Professor Schwartz was short in stature, his hair parted straight to the side, wore a little mustache, and reminded Alyssa of a Second World War character she had seen in her history book, but this man was brilliant, modern, up to date with all of what's going on in the American political arena.

"Well, class, that ends today's lecture. Want you to read and study next two chapters on the conflicting politics of the North and South leading up to the Civil War. We'll review how the American founding doctrine of cheap labor for a plantation society, in other words a nation founded on slavery, met some resistance in the smaller industrial Northern states and eventually sparked the armed conflict. Want you to tell me how President Lincoln reacted to all that. How did he play his politics? Okay, any questions?"

Alyssa quickly raised her hand even though what was on her mind was far from the Civil War. "Yes?" said Professor Schwartz looking directly at her near the front row.

"Sir, I know this is a more current question, and I know that it has taken us a long, long time to progress from the Civil War to our just society today, but if we have time could you just tell us how well the current political situation is progressing."

"Young lady, that is material for the last two weeks of this class ... but if you are having trouble sleeping..."

The twenty person class erupted into as simultaneous chuckle. The professor looked amused.

"Look, Alyssa, is your name? We are doing just fine. And you know this always happens. A few Justice Department lawyers get aggressive in order to advance their credentials, and they are looking into a corruption scandal of the Vice President and some others ... and a few other matters too, but I think we are doing just fine. We no longer are a republic of minority rule by a Senate comprised of equal votes, but we are a true democracy now. One man one vote. Each state only an influence by its population count. We continue to have a record voter turnout in all our federal elections. Everybody votes, but more importantly our extensive welfare legislation continues to roll along, and more..."

"Are we able to pay for all that?" she interrupted sheepishly, having a second thought about never interrupting a professor.

"Hey, that is out of this class. This is Political Science, not Finance. Young lady, I have answered your question. Any other questions before we end?" He seemed perturbed. The students looked at him in silence. Alyssa put her head down, not sure what to think next.

Tyler was alone with his thoughts that evening. He too was taking a political science class, but with a different professor than Dr. Schwarz. He also was taking a course in Sociology, a class whose teaching more recently was also really bothering him. *Why am I becoming so different,* he asked himself in silence. Finally calling it a night and knowing he was to be up early the next morning for his 8 a.m. history class, he tucked himself into bed. But he was restless. Sleep wouldn't come. Then he remembered the history books he found for himself in the university's extensive library. Some were quite different than what he was being taught in his political science class. Last year was American history and the emphasis on a slave economy. This year it was world history using textbooks fortunately not of recent origin. Classic political systems were all about the few who ruled and the masses who had no choice but to follow. Tribal leaders, Roman emperors, European kings, a thousand years of Russian czars, Mongolian warlords, and Japanese emperors ruling over in much greater numbers the peasants, serfs, and commoners. Political laws and religious rules became common beginning 3000 years ago for the purpose of keeping order among inherently disorderly man. But it wasn't the "people" who set the rules. Among the leaders, major disagreements were usually settled by war, armed conflict.

"Wow," he almost said out loud to himself. The so-called Enlightenment several hundred years ago then really changed things for the better. More men could participate in political discourse as they became more learned. Despite their king's supremacy, the Brits developed parliaments to discuss and resolve so many matters. Then the American founding fathers really got radically advanced. No king, no ruler, but an executive president with equal powers as the nation's elected legislative members, and a Supreme Court to resolve disputes. The political experiment worked even though it would take many years to bring women and minorities into the fold. The issues of those in favor of strong states' rights as the separate thirteen colonies broke ties from England were balanced with those educated leaders who saw the need for a strong federal system so that the new United States of America could have one currency not thirteen, one military to defend against foreign enemies, and one authority to promote free interstate commerce among the new states. To promote balance and democracy, the House of Representatives would serve short terms on behalf of their constituents based on population while the higher deliberative Senate members would serve longer terms based upon equality of the individual states. A nice compromise.

This sense of balance worked well for over two hundred years, yet Ty could not understand why this balance of power was now all so wrong. The elimination of equal Senate representation was being taught to us as the coming of true democracy, but some very smart people had warned of the "rule by the mob" concept. Deliberation and balance once good, now bad. Now the massive populations of Los Angeles and New York City, including their many voters not yet citizens nor competent in the English language and American customs, have massive political clout, that is, continuously reelecting their the so-called "leaders" supposedly representing them. America had become a land of one party rule. Its one party leaders always knowing what's best. Dissent was challenged, frowned upon, despised. The so-called free press was under their broad overreach. Ty was learning that social media leaders were rewarded for their adherence to the official political positions. The Justice Departments of the nation had a difficult time proving the growing, self-serving corruption of these so-called leaders, and seemed to be giving up. Entrenchment, big salaries, big benefits, favors, rewards – there was no way to reverse it. Political freedom, free speech, and individual worth had become subservient to political equality, a concept sounding good to the masses but one ending up with two unequal classes, the common man and the ever in office elected officials and their massive, well paid, loyal bureaucracy.

*Am I thinking too much?* he wondered. *Maybe I need complete darkness* to fall *asleep,* he thought to himself. He pushed the covers aside and rose to turn off the bathroom nightlight. 'Hypocrisy,' that's the word I'm thinking of I keep forgetting – orders of restriction expressed to others to do so-called 'good' for them, but then doing the opposite themselves – for their own benefit. *That's our self-centered, self-serving politicians.* He returned to his bed sensing a growing fatigue. Still, feeling the frustration, Tyler tossed and turned. He hoped he could trust his own research into all this that was bothering him. It took two more hours for him to doze off for the night.

*Power corrupts...*

# CHAPTER 2

★

## LIBERAL EDUCATORS

I t made no difference now. Grade school, junior high school, high school, college, graduate school, public school, private school – the teaching philosophy was all the same. It used to be called "progressive far left." Now it was called "progressive liberalism" – a classic phase now described as 'what's best for all'. Only the few remaining religious schools taught "conservatism" but that phrase, that ideology, was really out of style.

Tyler on this Friday had no other classes after his 8 a.m. Sociology. Still bothered by his tossing and turning the night before, he sought out the one person on campus who might give him solace. It was Professor Evans, a sixty-five year old scholar teaching English Literature to freshmen students. That was a course Ty took during the second semester of Ty's first year at Penn. Tyler was bothered by the seeming lack of enthusiasm the professor had displayed during his lectures. Never looking at any student in the eye, he seemed despondent, projecting a sense of wishing he wasn't even there. After class one day, Tyler approached his teacher and boldly inquired why with such interesting authors to discuss was the subject matter presented by him coming across as rather boring.

Professor Evans gave a quick look of surprise and then inquired. "You mean you like this stuff?" His eyes brightened at Tyler's response.

"Yes sir, I do. I find that behind these stories there is really an enlightenment going on here. George Eliot, really a woman author using a man's pen name, why her *Silas Marner* is astounding – how out of such bad fortune, eventually human bonding and happiness can be found. I loved the story, and that is just one example."

The professor's lips revealed a slight smile. His large blue eyes now transformed from their initial brightening to a look of amazement. "Young man, that's nice to hear. I would like to even hear more from you... Can you stop by my office at three this afternoon, if you are free?" And that initial interface was the start of multiple conversations between Tyler and Professor Evans over the ensuing months. It was revealed to Ty the man had lost his tenure, was going to be forced to retire at the end Tyler's sophomore year, that he was considered an outcast by his colleagues and university administrators because he had been viewed as a radical. He was that rare breed – a labeled 'political and intellectual conservative.' For the last ten years, he was viewed by his peers as unnecessary, useless, worthless. It was forbidden that he was to make any of his views publicly known.

Shortly after his encounter with Professor Evans and a day after his unpleasant 'debate' with Alyssa (Tyler rebelled against calling their debates 'arguments' since he loved her so much) he dropped in again on the professor. "Sorry, I know you will be leaving the university soon, and I sensed you have a feel for the movements of history from your literature classes, so I just wanted to..."

"No, no, please come in. Sit down, son. I'd love to chat some more with you. You know, you're a rare breed. Willing to gain a sense of history as to where we are today and which way we are headed. Anywhere you want to start."

"Yes, sir, social systems. Well, starting with the world of the intellectuals. And the world of the radicals. The energetic, outspoken ones seemed to have so much influence. From the books I found in the library, I read of the influence of people who wrote big stuff, like Adam Smith on capitalism during the 1700's and Karl Marx on Communism in the mid 1800's and then the influenced leaders like Thatcher, Reagan, Trotsky, Lenin, Stalin, Hitler, Mao, Castro, Chavez, ..."

"Tyler, yes the list is long. Many great writers had an influence on society's fortunes. The stress between free enterprise and socialism has long been with us. Even though Adam Smith believed that free enterprise produced wealth for the most, he preached that it had to have a strong moral grounding. Karl Marx, the founder of communism, 'from each according to his ability to each according to his needs,' believed the material world governed man's behavior and destiny and taught that the ongoing class struggle between the haves and the have nots was so paramount that only an armed revolution could solve the problem, and that once solved the socialist state could disappear and the working people would rule on their own. So, the intellectual class bought the latter argument for social justice but hoped it would occur without armed conflict. On the other side, early 'liberalism' was all about the worth of every man, his intellect, and his freedom from tyranny. This certainly appealed to the university class. Their occupation was to teach peace in their ivory towers, not go to war in the trenches.

"Some of them over the decades believed on holding on to values that seemed to work for the good of the most. They became known as 'conservatives,' but they were the minority in the intellectual class. Many capitalist leaders in the early days of free enterprise naturally were selfish, their basic human nature, and so the rise of labor unions and worker benefits were essential in balancing out the advancement. So, look back

– enlightened capitalism seemed to progress and be so beneficial to so many even though its precepts sounded so selfish, whereas communism and socialism, sounding so good, seemed to not only fail, but damaged so many... So, what's going on here? Tyler, you were not allowed to read this like students of thirty years ago did, but the pen-named author George Orwell wrote a short book in 1945 called *Animal Farm*. He was an advocate in Britain of enlightened democratic socialism but dreaded Russian dictatorial communism because its leaders became selfish and corrupt. In his novel the farm animals rid themselves of their human overlord, like the Russians did in 1917 of their czars, but in the end their own animal leaders become selfish and corrupt. You see, free enterprise takes hard work and individual responsibility whereas socialism implies a free ride but not understanding the eventual predominate human natural trait of self-interest. A bad ending in that novel, and you see that is exactly what is happening to America now. Our intellectuals believe in a utopian society. Their influence on the ruling class, the progressive Democratic Party, the elites, the bureaucracy, the social media, the high-tech industry, and now all the media – why it's overwhelming. My boy, what in the world are you doing here with me – this lone outcast?"

Tyler's eyes opened wide, his face turned to a look of awe, "I ... I don't know. I think I understand what you are saying. I've wanted to know for sure, I want to understand more. My great grandfather in Vladivostok, my friend Alyssa here. I want to understand right and wrong."

"There is no right and wrong Tyler. There are only the shifting sands of time. We humans have progressed from our cave man days. Nature controlled us over our centuries of progress. Disease, famine, storms predominated, but along with our wars, wars, wars, yet despite the natural obstacles and the flow of violently competing social and political systems, there are more of us now than ever. The introduction of agriculture and advanced medicine like vaccines, and new technologies, all allowed us to dominate. We are even trying now to control nature. We think we can bring the nature of the planet to a standstill. We are saving the planet now." Prof let out a half chuckle and then sat back and looked momentarily blank.

"But, sir, if there are more of us now because of advancing technologies of producing plentiful food and wiping out major diseases, are we not much better off? Should I really not worry about what's going on out there?"

Professor Evans shifted his eyes towards Tyler's inquiring eyes. There was silence in his office setting for several moments until he finally responded to Tyler's intelligent question. "Yes, yes you are right about our advancement, but not worry? No, you should worry, because we are now in decline in so many ways. Our happiness over the millennium of our human physical progress falls to the few who can find family, friends, rules, community, love, peace, prayer, and hope – all blessings to us individually at some point despite our collective chaos. I've had mine. It's now gone for me. You? Maybe you have to emigrate to New America where some of your family has gone. They have made a fresh start. Here, here we are in academic decline, a socialist mess. Free thought only for the leftist ideology in this once great university. Free to curse, free to condemn anyone who opposes, and the welcoming of free sex, free drugs, all blameless for any dirty deed. For years, educational vocations attracted the more liberal thinkers and there were few of us so called conservatives. Maybe it seemed less financially rewarding for we conservative bents to go into education, so the field didn't attract as many of us, but today we have gone from a small voice to no voice. We have been cancelled." His eyes dropped. His face expressionless.

"Professor Evans, I want to hear so much more, but sir, I have to run now. I do want to see you again before the end of the semester. You will be leaving then," Tyler replied despondently.

★

*Do as I say, not as I do.* An old, old saying.

# CHAPTER 3

──────── ★ ────────

## SOCIALISM

Friday night was finally here. It had been a grueling week for Tyler. His debate midweek with Alyssa, his Political Science class, his serious discussions with the somber Professor Evans, and his Sociology class today were all in sum mentally wearing. He was glad his Sociology prof was different than Alyssa's. He wouldn't want to see her face during that subject –- a course more of academic brainwashing than intellectual learning, or so it seemed to the newly learned Tyler. It was mid-March, still early in the spring semester and still fairly cool outside, so Tyler planned a romantic evening for the two in his cozy apartment. He found an old romantic comedy on his TV movie list for them. Relax, enjoy some wine with popcorn and pretzels, and refrain from even thinking about the outside world. And look forward to some very intimate kissing and touching after the flick.

The evening went exactly as planned. It even was a miracle he could find an enjoyable old Hollywood movie that had no violence, no sex, and no cursing – very difficult to find that anomaly in 2033. Even their display of affections, short of actual intercourse, of course, went well. Not even thinking about utilizing birth control methods since neither one wanted an accidental baby. They had made this waiting commitment despite most of their friends on some type of birth control pill. Well, this evening had all gone perfectly – until the end, just before walking her onto campus and to her dorm room.

"Oh Ty, you rascal, I do love you so much, but before we leave just one quick thought, I learned in my sociology class." She tilted her head to the side with her eyes wide open seeking his approval. "Please," she begged. "Sit, sit." The lights had been dimmed all evening, the couch and pillows so comfortable. What was to come simply did not match.

"Oh no," he said to himself slowly and reluctantly sliding back onto the couch. She went on without giving him a chance to say, "not tonight sweetheart,"

"So did you know some of those so-called Founding Fathers like Thomas Jefferson had sex with their slave girls and produced children. Of course, today mixed racial marriages are common, but at that time the blacks were the inferior race... Well, you men! Can you explain yourselves?" she exclaimed with a smile and a glance at his now sullen face. She went on nonstop. "So, as we know our history, we were founded by white Europeans as a slave society back in 1619. Big farms needed cheap labor. There was only a little bit of industry in the northern colonies early on so no slavery there. So, as society developed and industry grew, we became really two distinct societies. The big rich farms, the plantations in the South with free slave labor, black of course, and small farms and industry and commerce in the North. Women had no vote then so the politicians in the South were big landowners producing cotton for clothing and tobacco for smoking pleasure. The original Constitution, of course now updated to modern times, had stated all men are created equal, but that meant only men and only white men. With the North South split, hostilities were inevitable, and the two sides became armed blue and armed grey. Lincoln of course did not want to see the Southern states secede so in freeing the slaves he accepted there had to be war to preserve the Union. Well, let me tell you, it took a hundred years before our progressives advanced the freed slave to a degree of political freedom in our Civil Rights laws some sixty-five years ago."

Tyler wanted to stop this, but Alyssa continued right on. It was her turn to be on a roll.

"But behold Mister Tyler, for many years after, our country still had inequality among the races. We had systemic racism until we got the right people in political power and ended it. And we are making up for our past sins by the reparation laws passed ten years ago. We have created equity for the blacks. We have ended white supremacy. We have a perfect society now where everyone can look at each other in the eye and feel we are among equals. And the old problems in society with poverty and class distinctions and privileges – all gone now. We have ..."

"Stop, stop!" Tyler finally shouted, taking no more. "Alyssa, you are parroting the nonsense your professor spoon fed you today. This is not a classroom here. Do you really know what's going on out there?" He did not want this to happen tonight.

Alyssa bit her lip, showing her displeasure at his outburst. He cruelly had interrupted her. "Okay Mister Smarty-pants. "Go ahead if you're so smart. I'll listen to your nonsense."

Tyler calmed himself and realized he had no chance to end the debate. "Okay, okay. I hate this bickering, so I'll try to be brief, okay? You tell me when to stop. I've heard your side spout out how fair our society is now, but look outside and learn. I wasn't sure what to think a year ago, but I've learned. I've learned where to look for facts not misinformation. I know where to get the true information now. Yes, we agree we have advanced to political freedom among the classes and races and freedom before the law. We all wanted that. The blacks got the vote way back in 1965. But don't forget America was always the mixing pot. We have all the world's races and nationalities here, not just black and white. One would think blacks originally from Africa were 50% of the population. They are only 13%. Asians, Arabs, Hispanics, blacks, and whites, all the religions Christian, Jews, Muslims, Buddhists, all of them. We are a big mix especially with more intermarriage of races and religions and even more with the decline in formal marriages, a growing intermix. Fine, but social and economic equality, Alyssa? That's a joke. You have to look outside these ivy-coated walls.

"So, the poor get an educational opportunity, but their schools are grossly inferior, lack of quality teachers despite their incredible union benefits, high crime neighborhoods overflowing with drugs and crime, free health care but a decline in quality medicine with under-motivated health care providers. They get into college now everywhere but only the few brightest eventually succeed. And classless now? Ha! The elites in the business world, in the entertainment world, in the government world – they have the money and benefits beyond compare. And they show it – the way they live, their comfortable lives. Their unannounced but obvious air of superiority shows clearly, knowing what's best for the rest. Natural competition among and between people shows up just as much as the traits of compassion and cooperation. Most of us still behave to our best advantage. If it's easy to become corrupt to achieve that, then it happens. Except for a few, we have become a lazy society with only a few really contributing. Our political leaders are self-serving, content, and corrupt, and they provide us with only empty promises towards the perfect society. And meanwhile the cost for this great society has ballooned to the point where even the richest have not been taxed enough to pay for it... "

"Okay, enough." Alyssa said quietly, raising her hand to Tyler's lips. "If we are going to get along, Ty, as a couple, you would have to take me out in the streets and show me what you are talking about. No one else talks like you do. I'm, I'm ... Take me back now to my dorm," she said softly, Ty detecting a tear rolling down from her eye. Maybe she was now in a confused state as he was a year ago.

The fifteen minute walk back to Alyssa's residence hall was in silence, holding hands but no conversation. The streets were empty, except for the ubiquitous campus security detail, for crime in the outside city was rampant. A short kiss goodnight, and that was it. No words.

Walking back to his apartment, Tyler was beginning to feel somewhat depressed. A great evening with this beautiful young woman was now in ruins. Thoughts rambled through his head about where he believed his nation now stood socially. What had been initially promised as Democratic Socialism by the so-called progressive left was really a repeat of history. America was not the very limited society of Denmark, a nation of only five million homogeneous people occupied in World War II by Nazi Germany but mostly one escaping the bloodbath of other Nazi occupied nations. Nonetheless, the war's horrors meant the common people wanted fairer societies, and the rise of so-called democratic socialism became more popular among voting classes. The ordinary people were willing to pay high income taxes, average forty-five percent, and high sales taxes, twenty-five percent in order to pay for greater social and security benefits. The busy prosperous ports along the coast also contributed to the national income, along with the carryover benefit of the wealthy aristocrats, behind the scenes now, but still taxpayers of the ones left. Very different and easier to implement in little Denmark after World War II than in diverse

America founded on the principles of individualism and limited government.

But the implementation of 'Denmark' in the United States in 2021 soon went far beyond the democratic socialism of Denmark. In its true sense, socialism means government control or ownership of the nation's means of production. This concept had progressed in England after World War II until its gross inefficiencies were reversed by Margaret Thatcher in the 1980's. It was now Americas turn to repeat the economic socialist mistakes of England, Russia, China, Cuba, and Venezuela. From the period running 2021 to now 2033, Tyler went over in his mind all the industries now owned, controlled or dominated by the state and federal governments. The omissions, the inefficiencies, the investigations through the growing number of official inquiries being set up to 'inquire' about the government's problems seemed to grow daily. The 'inquiries' never corrected the problems but did create multiple jobs and news stories.

Again, Tyler had difficulty falling asleep that night. Thank goodness he thought, he could at least look forward to a weekend of having fun with his best buddies playing tag football, basketball and watching golf on TV with some beer in hand.

Yes, Lord Acton, you were right.

*Power corrupts, and absolute power corrupts absolutely.*

# CHAPTER 4

———— ★ ————

# BANISHED DISSENT
# RACISM ENDED

## U.S. SOCIETY 2033

From his weekend's vigorous activities where no social or political subjects came up, Tyler woke up Monday morning feeling refreshed. He knew he faced the dreaded Sociology class again at 10 a.m. and thank goodness that he and Alyssa were not in the same class. He vowed he was just going to be upbeat this day. As usual on Monday mornings, he met Alyssa at 9:30 for a cup of coffee on their way to their classes. He tried his best to be pleasant with her, how good she looked and how sorry he was they couldn't get together Saturday evening.

Associate Professor Evelyn Warner was very pleasing to look at and listen to. She was fairly young looking, a nice voice, and told her class at the outset she was Black African American, even though her skin color was a rather light brown. Today's subject she started by saying, "Listen up everybody. We have covered so many subjects lately, and I have been kind of lecturing a little too much, so today let's open it up to your questions. Anybody ... start." The twenty some students looked startled at first then rather pleased. Miss Warner had been a good lecturer with her pleasant demeanor, but this seemed a welcome change.

An Asian appearing girl in the front row opened with "Miss Warner, I know as a society we have achieved a situation of diversity and inclusion. That's good, right? I, myself, I feel lucky to be here, but my grandfather lives with us, and he keeps asking me why there are no Opinion pages anymore in the newspapers he reads or on the television stations he watches. Can you..."

"Certainly, Kim, we hear that a lot, but the short answer is that we are now a true democracy, and we don't need to hear radical voices anymore. We have free speech guaranteed to us, but we weed out right wing characters who are even willing to commit violence to protect what they think are the opposites of diversity and inclusion. They probably wish for the old days of white supremacy."

The joy of the day just ended for Tyler. He simply couldn't resist jumping in. With his bold, clear voice, he spoke up, "Excuse me, when I hear the words 'white supremacy' – I know that was a big issue ten years ago and from the founding of our nation, but **my** grandfather tells me there was Persian, Babylonian, and Egyptian supremacy for a while then white supremacy with the Greeks and the Romans, then Arab supremacy for a while with the spread of Islam, then Asian supremacy for a while with the spread of the Mongolian Empire, then the white Western Europeans got educated, developed better weapons and ocean going ships than all the others so they naturally became supreme as they spread themselves around the world developing their colonies and increasing their wealth. So, hasn't the history of civilization always been one of conflict between tribes, countries, and races each antagonistic trying to get one up on the other?"

"Exactly, young man. Tyler, is it? That's the tremendous progress we have made here in America as a society. Moving past all that discrimination to a more perfect society where everybody is the same. All our diverse peoples are now included. There is no more racism, no more white supremacy ..."

"Excuse me, Miss Warner, but why then, and we are all in favor of no more discrimination, did we have to fill in those question-naires at the start of the semester whether we are Asian, Black, White, Hispanic ... when so many of us have a mixed heritage and we all are one now, yet we are classified constantly whether in schools or jobs what race we are. We live by our identities. There are smart Asians with strong family influences who are denied entry into top colleges. There is reverse discrimination everywhere." Tyler's voice grew louder, his face showing his heightened emotions.

"Why can't we drop all that and just all **assimilate** into one American society," he nearly screamed, then caught himself and sat back. The student next to him squirmed uncomfortably in her seat, but interesting that two black students near the front row turned around and nodded approvingly towards Tyler. Professor Warner seemed momentarily lost for words. The Asian girl in the front row spoke up again, somewhat sheepishly but emboldened hearing this boy Tyler speak up for Asians.

"Yes, I would like to add to his remarks. It's not only that I am referred to all the time as a Korean Asian and my best friend as a Black African, but we are also constantly grouped into our sexual orientation and preference despite we all being equal. Are you gay, are you a transsexual, a lesbian, are you a member of LGBTQ Community and going to this group meeting or that? I like what he said about our just assimilating as Americans, accepting each other without identity labels, and speaking only English in public and any heritage languages at home." The classroom was momentarily silent.

A trembling thought raced through Tyler's mind. *We are each addressed by our identity, but we are all the same. Are we all equal but some are more equal than others?*

Evelyn Warner's body language hinted towards a look of being uncomfortable as it seemed 'free speech' had suddenly gotten out of hand. "Look, this is not up for debate. So many of us have grandfathers, great grandfathers raised as inferiors. I have some from once slave families. After we were freed from slavery, we had a long history of repression and violence. Even 'separate but equal' didn't work. Then we got civil rights like voting rights, affirmative action programs, became mayors of big cities, even a president of the United States, but systemic racism went on. Blacks being shot needlessly by white cops. All that is over now. And we even have reparations being paid to black families in need."

Tyler was holding his breath. It seemed useless to argue, but then a tall black student in the back of the class stood up and quietly but clearly spoke these words. "I appreciate your saying all that, Miss Warner, but I too have grandfathers who have seen all sides of this. But they too are silenced now. One considered himself an intellectual, black conservative. Not allowed now. He feels that that official racism has ended, but that fact has not helped our people out in the streets. He believed the black community had to stand up for itself and commit to pulling themselves out of their hole with their own responsibility, hard work and effort, socially and economically. The so-called advancement has only helped the elite blacks, those with connections, great educations, or picked out for advancement.

"We have more drug use now than ever. The legalization of so many harmful drugs may have added tax revenues and taken some drug dealers off the streets, but the fact is use has gone up, our people addicted become lazy, and the big increase in drug addition programs can't keep up in quality or quantity.

And crime. We don't have white cops shooting young blacks anymore, which was very small statistically anyway, but the lack of jobs in so many areas, the lack of discipline, the inferior schools, the huge number of guns out there despite guns other than strict hunting guns now banned. I read there are almost 400 million civilian guns in the United States, more than our population. There is no way to round them all up. Blacks killing blacks still goes on. Gangs, random shootings. The big cities report the numbers since so many wind-up dead or in the hospital. Hundreds, into the thousands. And suicides – among us blacks now too. The number increases every year... so I consider myself lucky. I got into this great university on a need scholarship because I had pretty good grades in high school. My mother and father both lived at our home, not so common in my community, along with two of my grandparents. I read a lot of books, sort of like that poor guy who became a great surgeon, Ben Carson I think was his name. The boy paused, realizing maybe he had been talking too long, but his classmates seemed mesmerized. Tyler broke into a slight smile as he turned his attention back towards Miss Warner. Even the student next to him now sat still, seemingly spellbound.

"All right. Enough for today," Evelyn Warner sighed. "These open discussions have to be controlled so we can stay on subject, which is the systematic analysis of our citizens' behavior acting collectively. That's what sociology is. We won't have time for individual stories again. So, let's move on to Chapter Twelve in your textbooks and let's just start reading to yourselves. That will give you a jump on your next homework assignment."

Tyler thought of Alyssa in her Sociology class. If she had listened to all of this, he sensed she would have a cold look in her eye, and that he would have stared back at her with a blank face. The two went their separate ways after their respective classes, Alyssa to her next class in the same building, Tyler with an hour to kill before his next class in a different hall. He walked slowly outside and sat down alone on a bench, thinking, thinking about the real nature of his society outside this well maintained, highly secure university sanctuary. Homeless tents seemed ubiquitous both in the city and outside it, as did petty crime. Stealing was no longer punishable nor was there prosecution for any property damage associated with it. Serious crimes such as murder were investigated and prosecuted by a small unit within the governments' Community Assistance Departments, or CAD, found in every governmental jurisdiction. These units were small and lacked sufficient personnel to effectively enforce any crimes except the most grievous.

Tyler remembered as a kid seeing men and women in uniform with guns showing on their waists. They were called 'police.' Now that such departments were defunded and disbanded and their physical locations now part of the CAD network, guns only seemed to be heard and not seen. Four hundred million of them, all illegal except certain hunting rifles. He understood the main activity of CAD was to provide mental health assistance and drug addiction assistance to anyone in need. Those needs he learned were gigantic, and there were simply not enough trained, motivated, and competent personnel to do the job effectively, no matter how noble the purpose. He shuttered – *Is this what Alyssa is training to do?*

He closed his eyes for a moment, trying to visualize something good going on in his life. He couldn't. His mind raced to the marijuana he had been offered by his buddies Saturday night. Recreational use now legal everywhere, in all fifty-two states, but the impact to him seemed positive only to the elderly retired population. In that segment, he had read the cost of Medicare healthcare had declined by a huge margin as a result of providing free medical marijuana to all those over age sixty-two. A great concept, as all old people need medical assistance at some point. Such savings of course could in no way begin to reduce the huge skyrocketing costs of the federal government's Universal Healthcare for those under the age of sixty-two. He recalled his friend John Saturday night hinting that he might try cocaine since there are no penalties for buying and using it, and that it might give him more of a 'kick' than pot. Tyler's response had been negative. "Forget it, John. Man, we know how lazy this stuff has made so many of us, but that stronger stuff becomes so additive so quickly that it's life destroying. You must know how big it's become a problem for our society. Man, don't even think about it. It can only harm you." Tyler recalled John just staring off as if not even hearing Tyler's stern admonition.

Tyler glanced at his watch. Fifteen more minutes to next class, Spanish, a two minute walk. He tried to envision his Wednesday night date with Alyssa, common this semester since neither had a morning class on Thursdays. But his mind inexorably went back to his thinking about American society. He started to remember the research he had done. Suicides in America were some 40,000 per year back at the turn of the century, to nearly 50,000 by 2020, and up to 75,000 per year by 2030. There were just so many people who felt they could not cope with an increasingly complex society or frustrating life or an inability to deal with relationships. So many reasons but the increase well beyond the increase in population was disturbing. He then remembered violent crime, nearly 400,000 cases in 2020 with nearly 20,000 murders to some 600,000 in 2030, although so many not reported to the CAD's by that time, with almost 40,000 murders per year by 2030. Tyler's mid raced to drugs. He remembered his findings. Some 75,000 deaths to drug overdose in 2020 skyrocketing to over 100,000 by 2030. And the numbers so high for the once illicit drugs now common in society that by 2033 there are no sources to account for how high are the numbers of current users. Opioids, cocaine, heroin, marijuana - all so common now.

Another mind rush stirred Tyler. *The government takes care of everybody, but while the elites prosper, the masses suffer. This just doesn't match.*

He rose quickly from the bench and raced to his Spanish class. Thankfully, the late morning air was brisk and the sky clear. 'Enough' he said to himself clearing his head.

*All men are equal, but some men are more equal than others.*

# CHAPTER 5

★

## GOVERMENTS' SPENDING BINGE

Wednesday evening was going to be different. Tyler privately decided in advance there would be no talk of society's ills. Alyssa to herself had done the same. There was to be no talk of society's advancements and then have Tyler dispute it all. It was nearly halfway through the two's second semester, the end of March when Spring would soon be in the campus air. They met at Nigel's, a quaint bar and casual restaurant at the edge of campus. It was located at the limit of the university's vast security detail established to protect its faculty and students from the high crime rates of neighboring areas. They had fun together, enjoying a pasta and wine dinner, listening to the trio onstage playing decent jazz, laughing together at almost any comment. Afterwards, the two walked hand in hand back to Alyssa's dorm, a long kiss goodnight, a warm embrace. *This is how it should be,* Tyler thought to himself as he walked briskly back to his apartment. Alyssa entered her room thinking *why can't he always be like this.*

Once a week, at 11 a.m. on Thursdays Tyler attended a class at Penn's business school, the highly acclaimed Wharton School. The elite school had come a long way, from a nearly all white, all male student and faculty body seventy-five years before to a very integrated population, including now even a very talented and renowned black woman Dean. Tyler's class was entitled

Government and Corporate Finance. His instructor was an Associate Professor named Joshua Gerber. "Let's get it straight, class, I don't take sides. I'm not an economic philosopher nor an advocate of anything political in this course. I'm here just to teach you facts." Tyler clearly remembered this statement because as the semester went on, there was so much controversy among the economists willing to speak out, the press, the business community, and the politicians as to the appropriate amount of money local, state, and federal governments should be spending. This prof wanted no part of that debate.

It only seemed smart for Tyler to spend an hour in Penn's massive library an hour before each week's class trying to research and study the history of industries and governments' roles in the developing American economy. It seemed America had thrived on free enterprise and private business growth for generation upon generation, but always those recessions every few years as business people would get too optimistic, then over-inventory their goods, and then have to back off until the next growth spurt. Then the major Depression of 1929 caused by excessive greed and major over exuberance setting economic growth back until the second World War period of the early 1940's. Seems like free market capitalism had its shortcomings.

All the while governments expanded their reach, but especially the federal government which did not have to balance its budget. Local governments had been established to provide basic protection such as police and fire, help with construction of bridges and roads to facilitate transportation, and establish and fund schools for public education. All done staying within a budget based on local tax revenues. State governments did the same on a broader scale, as for instance adding state health departments and institutions and requiring various regulatory licenses to do business within the state. To assist in financing these growing functions, many states introduced state income and sales and inheritance taxes, but again on a balanced budget requirement. Both cities and states also issued municipal bonds to raise money, attractive to investors because their interest income was granted a tax-free status. Not until granting excessive future benefits to public employees, like their pension plans, did the trouble begin. By 2030 there were so many cities and states unable to fund retirement benefits that recourse was made to the federal government for so called 'bail outs.'

Now we are in trouble, Tyler read in some of the out of style economic writings. The mainstream publications would not issue such stern remarks. Over time the federal government had overextended its reach. The national armed forces, the assurance of free commerce among the states, the management of some federal lands for national parks, the assurance of one sound money system were not enough. No one but the feds could break up the huge monopolies some industries had formed. The feds had to assure competition in the business community to keep prices down for the public. Then as a result of high unemployment during the Great Depression of the 1930's only the federal government could provide benefits like work programs and retirement income. How could they do this? By the fact the federal government did not in its Constitution require a balanced budget. It could sell it securities. It could print money. It could spend more than it took in with its tax revenue. It could raise the tax rates as high as it wanted. The highest marginal rate even went to ninety percent to help finance the Second World War.

For decades the economic debates raged. Lower tax rates would stimulate the national economy, provide for more jobs and taxpayers and everyone would be better off versus the converse – no, let's tax the rich, they can afford it, and under the welfare clause we can expand benefits to all, like free universal healthcare, free higher education, greater childcare benefits, higher unemployment benefits, pension benefits including helping states and municipalities with their underfunding. Tyler noticed a paragraph in one economics book written in 2020 that the national debt reached $20 trillion by 2018 then up to $27 trillion by the end of 2020, increasing dramatically from the turn of the century 2000. There had been the pandemic spending in 2020 and 2021, but with the advent of one party rule, the progressive left wing party had pushed the national debt to nearly $40 trillion by 2033.

"Mr. Gerber, I don't understand." A hand went up in the back of the classroom. "Could you could explain how the Unites States finances its annual deficits. You said the high tax rates on the income of the rich and the wealth tax upon their assets are not doing enough. And with over fifty percent of workers paying no income taxes, why isn't the national sales tax that started in 2024 raising enough money?" Tyler looked on intently. His pre-class research had not covered that circumstance.

"Okay, let's review again," answered Mr. Gerber. The federal government issues debt, federal Treasury notes and bonds, as it borrows to finance its programs beyond what it takes in with tax revenues. Rarely has the federal government balanced its annual budget in the last one hundred years. The growing deficit has not been a major concern to most when viewed as a percentage of the national economy. It's increased, yes, but not too much according to most government economists. The debt is held over thirty percent by foreigners, investors, banks, and governments. As the world's second leading economy behind China, we are deemed a safe risk. Who buys the near seventy percent? Some one third of it is bought by revenues brought into various government trust funds, like Social Security. The rest is split between private investors, retirement funds, and the like on the one side and our Federal Reserve Bank on the other. That portion is usually granted as credit to its member banks increasing the nation's money supply to finance economic growth. So, it all works out, and we are not too concerned as long as the economy doesn't become over stimulated and have excessive inflation appear as a result." Despite his plea of impartiality, Professor Gerber looked a little uncomfortable.

The student went on. "But sir, with the very slow growth of the economy the last ten years and with rising interest rates the government has to currently pay out, isn't it a concern that eventually those trust funds have to be paid back, that it's giant China buying most of the foreign held debt now. My father in manufacturing said American industry is being squeezed out, and that government overspending for every this and that has no discipline attached to it. That it's no wonder that unemployment is rising, that prices are soaring ..."

"Hear me," Mr. Gerber said raising his voice. "We are not getting into opinions. We are not here to mull the past, present or future. Only to review the numbers, the facts. This is the national debt number, the tax revenues, the deficit number, how it's financed." He paused and looked down for a moment. He remembered he had used the word "concern" just moments earlier. Tyler squirmed in his seat. *This was major*, he thought to himself. Any controversy allowed to be spoken of out loud are the ongoing debates among the liberal economists, the liberal press, and the liberal politicians only about how big the next year's government spending should be among all the multiple government programs. Each was competing vocally for a bigger appropriation. Tyler thought *Craziness!* He left the classroom scratching his head.

*Borrow and spend; spend more and borrow more.*
The Storyteller

# CHAPTER 6

★

## FREE HEALTH CARE

In addition to "free' education through government where not only elementary and secondary education was provided to all, whether citizens or not [originally locally controlled and financed within budget through property taxes] by 2033 any and **all** education desired by any individual was provided for, worthy or not academically, financed through federal government borrowing.

Tyler found himself free Thursday night, a perfect evening to knock on Professor Evans door again. He just could not get this idea out of his mind of unlimited, unrestrained concept of government spending beyond tax revenues. He needed some historical perspective, and Professor Evans seemed so grounded.

"Yes, sure, come in Tyler. You are always welcome. Glad you found my humble dwelling. Not many I can chat with these days." The words flowed with sincerity but little enthusiasm. Doctor Evans, as he was known among the university faculty for having his Ph.D. in Literature, lived in a small but nicely furnished apartment just across the Schuylkill River from the Penn campus. Tyler had found the address from one of their prior meetings in his on-campus office. He immediately noticed one wall of the living room was completely taken up from side to side from floor to ceiling of a huge bookcase completely full. This was a very well read college prof, Tyler reasoned.

"Have a cup of tea, or a beer, young man? I'm just finishing up my last glass of wine."

"Oh, no thank you, Professor, I'm fine. Just had a big dinner," Tyler responded showing a nice smile.

"Okay, fine, so what brings you out this evening for this visit? Not that I don't know. You are a very inquisitive lad about what's going on in this once great country. Right?" grinned the usually sullen Prof.

"Well, yes, I wanted to get your opinion on healthcare. From what I'm hearing from a med school friend of mine, he's found his initial choice of vocations not looking so promising now. He said his aging father really had it great. Long, long hours and hard work as a physician but very rewarding personally ... and financially too. He was really admired for helping so many people, always learning more about the human body, disease, healing, good health habits ... generous with his time, and well paid so he could advance his children, give to charity, enjoy his limited time off. My friend said..."

"Whoa," said the Prof interrupting Tyler. "You have said a mouthful there. Yes, there is a past, and there is a present. Was your friend misled, do you think, into thinking being a physician was going to be a rewarding career?" From the amusement of a curious student dropping in on him for a casual discussion to now a more serious matter, Doctor Evans' facial expression turned to one of surprise and anticipation. Then he remembered this boy Tyler was always in deep thought about his society each time they had met back on campus.

"Well, I'm not sure. I think he actually was discouraged by his father from even going to med school, but my friend had heard so much about we all need to be civil servants, helping out everyone. The words were 'unselfish,' 'empathetic.' But now he is hearing so much about what's really going on from doctors, nurses, health care workers, he's getting confused... I guess I'm just curious. What were we then, what are we now?"

"Understood, Tyler. Okay, let's go back. Now remember you are conversing with a relic here. My conservative views are out of style now, you know that. And I'm a literature instructor, you know that, but I know you want to hear the other side too, so let's go.

"Long ago," the Prof spoke slowly, softly, deliberately, "the ancient doc's understood how complex the human body was. How hard to heal so many times with so many infirmities and diseases... Once microorganisms were discovered and that some caused illness and even death, ways were introduced to vastly improve sanitary conditions. Then, once vaccines were invented, many contagious diseases were virtually wiped out, like deadly smallpox and crippling polio. Then some seventy years ago, the human genome was discovered and our DNA laid out, 'mapped' they called it. Tremendous advances followed scientifically, but medical practice still remained very much an art as well as a science. Why? Because the great complexity of the human body was still there, along with the new understanding that in each human body, the chemistry, the detail, can be slightly different person to person. Diagnosis of a problem can still be quite difficult even with all the new imaging technology. The newer biotechnology industry has made tremendous advances in understanding and in treatments, but the battle goes on. There are billions of tiny viruses out there we have not yet identified or understand their potential capability for attacking humans as hosts and causing epidemics and pandemics. So, it seems at some point in every person's life, there is a need for a doctor, a nurse, even a hospital, particularly as we age.

"So, the field of medicine was, and is, so universally needed, so much in demand, that our brightest and most talented have taken to the call. Physicians were needed, highly respected, and accordingly in the cities and suburbs amply rewarded financially. It was an esteemed profession ... until some fifteen years ago.

"You know young man, there is so much controversy here, so much conflict in healthcare thinking, just like there is in so many other areas. When I was your age and so enthusiastic about learning, I thought that 'reason' would always prevail despite the so many differences and stupid things we young teachers witnessed. Resolution would eventually occur. It wasn't long after when I came to the conclusion that hoping and praying for harmony was just wishful thinking. Unending conflict is just part of our human condition. The medical profession is now a mess."

Tyler sat completely still, spellbound. *How could this professor of literature know so much?* He thought for a moment about his grandmother before she ventured to New America. She had a battle with cancer, and the top university bioethicists were trying to convince the government that people over sixty-five years of age should not be treated for serious illnesses. It was just too expensive. The government response had been that everyone gets treated, eventually that is, that rationing care was the unofficial policy to keep the soaring costs of universal healthcare down, and that medical marijuana for all the aged would also help. Thank goodness she survived on her own.

The two stand up lamps in the room were set on low, the one table lamp on slightly brighter, but still the professor's whole room appeared to be glowing while the reflection on the professor's face was alive, a perfect portrait of a man in deep thought. Tyler remained quiet, waiting, wanting to hear more. The prof took the final sip of red wine from his glass, and continued, looking off towards his massive bookcase. It was though he was on camera, casting verbal reflections out to his books of learning. After this long pause, the prof spoke on.

"I too have friends in this field, Tyler lad. Don't see them anymore. Too depressing... So, when Medicare came along over fifty years ago to take care of the medical needs of seniors over the age of sixty-five and Medicaid to take care of the medical needs of the indigent, the programs were never sufficiently funded to pay for themselves, that happening despite the very modest twenty-five year deficit projections at the time of enactments. So, guess what? Even after all the tax revenues were counted plus the small fees paid by those served, the costs soared way above the revenues by 2020, by about a trillion dollars, the huge growing deficits financed through low payments to medical providers and the outside financing of the government deficit. In the hole back then by a trillion dollars a year was of no concern to our wonderful politicians taking care of the voters. Nor was it a concern to them that while the programs were hugely popular with our retired folks and our poor folks, the medical community was taking a financial beating initially saved only by the higher premiums required by the younger based private market run by private based companies, insurance companies and unions.

Then ten years ago, the concept of Universal Healthcare finally won out, not a neat system like required health insurance at birth for everyone through the nationwide availability of some twenty-five different competitive, internet available, private plans with government premium assistance only for the truly needy ... but rather this magnificent Medicare for All, solely financed and managed by the federal government. So, guess at the result we have now."

Tyler squirmed in his wooden armchair, one surely not as pleasant as the professor's large leather chair where the teacher looked quite so comfortable. Doctor Evans continued to look out past Tyler towards his very large library. The prof's pause, or was it a question? In any case, a moment for Tyler to push on. "Yes, I understand. Okay, got it. So, from all that, what do we have now? Inefficiency in management, underfunded health care providers?" Tyler's brow raised, his eyes opened wide.

"What do we have now. It's a question. What do we have now? What we have now is a medical profession stuck in gloom. Over worked, underpaid. Doctors, nurses, physician assistants, aides – heck they are all disillusioned. Everyone on the planet has a medical problem or a complaint, some people every day. There are not enough of them, the health providers I mean, and they are not motivated. The politicians never thought of that angle. So, we are ending up with poor medical practices, a massive inefficient bureaucracy, a mounting federal deficit – all without concern. After all, the politicians hide the facts and tell you they are raising the tax revenues. The public has no concern because they have no payments to make. Oh yes, the higher income tax rates on the rich, the ever increasing wealth tax on them, the new federal sales tax, the rate inching up each year – none of that can finance the deficit spending on this program. So, if the waiting rooms get overcrowded at the doc's office or at the hospital, millions of people now get overlooked, some with serious conditions. The word nobody is allowed to use is "rationing." Some medical ethicists are getting their way and just saying no one over the age of seventy-five gets treated. Let 'em die. Or if the waiting line gets too long, maybe they will just go away. But many others will wait, and see a tired doc or over-worked assistant. And abortions on demand, to anyone, free to the would-be mother and hardly any money to the abortionist… Any dissent to the system, any other approaches, from the progressive thinking about any of this is no longer tolerated. We have been shut down." The professor finally rested from his long monologue. Without his own facial expression, he peered over towards Tyler's inquisitive face.

Tyler took his cue. "I follow you, but my question would be, sir. I am told we generally have a society that works much less hard than previous generations. We also have so many drug addicts with laziness the first affliction. We have a cradle to the grave welfare system that supposedly takes care of everybody. We have guaranteed annual income for everyone, working or not working. So, some would say --why are the healthcare workers working so hard? Just hire more to relieve the burden." Tyler showed a sudden look of remorse as he nearly bit his lip. He already knew the answer to that dumb question. "Wait..."

Professor Evans was quick to interrupt even though sensing Tyler knew the answer. "Fun, huh, young man. So, think about it. I'm sure you are getting the other side of the story too. Can you find the truth?"

Tyler responded with a grin. "That's what I'm after. Both sides of the story. I have a girlfriend, a person I admire so much... Well, she is on the side of the sociologists, the politicians. She is convinced everyone is now better off than before, or at least on the way to being better off. But I don't think she knows much about healthcare. Her mother is a high school teacher and her father a journalist. I guess you would say socially and politically both 'progressive liberals.' But what I'm getting into my noggin over and over again is that despite their wonderful intentions of equality, inclusion, diversity, equity, welfare, it seems in reality, in practice, it doesn't work out. If there is not the incentive for talented people who have to study hard, learn a lot, and apprentice hard over many years to be properly compensated one way or another for all that, then the caliber of those workers suffers. Good people will not be attracted to medical careers. There is no reward for merit. So, we can hire more, but at a much lower standard. The quality disappears. They are all now government employees. We must have so many trained, hard working, talented healthcare providers out there now who are so strained, but in another ten or twenty years what's the difference between working at the hospital or grilling hamburgers?" The two had said it all.

——— ★ ———

*If the care is free, I'll take it. Who cares what it cost?*

# CHAPTER 7

★

# DRUGS

John Frazier was a twenty-one year old junior at Penn when he met Tyler as an incoming freshman at a friendly informal tag football match on campus. He had become a terrific mentor for the young freshman. Now a senior and just a few short months to graduation, he is the one who was constantly suggesting to Tyler each time they got together for fun athletic games to try smoking pot, recreational marijuana now legal in all fifty-two states. Sensing how lazy it was making so many of his acquaintances, Tyler had consistently refused. Sure, the majority could handle it fine, just like alcohol, but that still left a huge growing minority. As for John, it was learned that his grade average had steadily dropped through his sophomore and junior years. He had even become quite lethargic in the ongoing tag football games. What was worse for Tyler were the constant hints about sniffing cocaine powder, which Tyler had warned his friend against. The stimulant drug was not exactly legal to sell but its use easily available and was not punishable.

On the Saturday after his meeting with Professor Evans on the topic of healthcare, there was to be another fun tag football match in the late afternoon followed by a stag dinner and drinks at a popular restaurant bar on the edge of campus. But it was raining heavily, and the game was called off with a text message to get to the bar earlier. When Tyler arrived, he was shocked to see John carrying on shouting and singing. Another friend, already high on smoking pot, cornered Tyler and whispered in Ty's ear that friend John had shot himself up with cocaine. "Hey Ty boy, that is a much stronger way than the crack powder he used to sniff." And then his friend laughed.

Tyler was taken back. This was no joking matter. He recoiled against the nearby wall with a look on his face of shock, of disappointment, of sadness. This was the guy who had taken him in so warmly a year and a half ago, showed him the ropes, the campus, the coed dorms. Like a big brother. Ty had often read about, had witnessed so much on campus, of the ease of getting and using stimulant drugs throughout American society. He had learned that there were so many drug addicts throughout all layers of society that there were not enough qualified caretakers to help them sufficiently. And now his best friend on campus? Tyler had even read that heavy usage of cocaine could lead to heart attack or stroke, even sudden death. What to do?

Unfortunately, he soon learned that there was nothing he could do. Private talks, referring him to Student Health, guidance counseling, requesting professors' interventions – nothing stopped John's spiral downhill. Graduation was now in jeopardy. Tyler began researching drug addiction through daily internet searches. He discovered there were few articles from any type of government sources but lots from independent sources. The problem was huge. All layers of society were impacted, but those whose income was protected by government jobs and union jobs felt the negative impact less. Nationalized health care was to help all, but the limited supply of qualified drug addiction workers and the futility of many of the prescribed programs were proving inadequate. And as Tyler had witnessed before, widespread usage prior to severe addiction was creating a society of simply lazy people. The result was more and more dependence on a federal government administering a bigger and bigger inefficient welfare state dependent on borrowing more and more money.

After all the guys had eaten their dinners and the beer continued flowing, Tyler took a second to glance at his watch. He knew Alyssa would be waiting for his call as to the timing they would later get together. He thought he should say goodbye to John and try to give him just one more warning. Not so easy he thought because John now really seemed out of it. Grabbing John's shoulder, he got close to his friend's ear. "John, John, listen to me. What you are doing is not right. Get off this strong stuff and back to beer. You know, you're going to jeopardize your graduation. "I want you…"

"Ty, old buddy, **you** listen up," John abruptly interrupted. "I don't care anymore. We are in a prison here," he stammered, barely coherent. "Campus security is everywhere caging us in, but we are not supposed to wander out, can't go off campus. Crime is everywhere. Drug dealers everywhere offering deals. What the hell am I going to do after graduation anyway? I didn't major in computer science so I could get a big job. I'm nothing in this stupid society," he sputtered out nearly falling off his seat. Tyler looked on and listened, helpless was his feeling.

———— ★ ————

*Eat, drink, and be merry for tomorrow we die. Smoke, sniff, and be merry for tomorrow we all die.*
Old and new expressions.

# CHAPTER 8

★

## MEDIA DISINFORMATION

Lots of exams and study time for both Tyler and Alyssa the following week so they decided to forego any weeknight get together and wait until Saturday afternoon and evening. Tyler was willing to give up his usual tag football game and beer-drinking frolic with his male friends. He felt somewhat depressed anyways as he learned his pal John would not be showing up. And Alyssa, if only they would concentrate on having fun together and not engage in any serious discussions. But again, thinking twice, he knew down deep that he had to convince her that this new society was not working and a joint move to New America was the salvation.

It was beautiful Spring afternoon, so Tyler rented a car for the day and had Alyssa's enthusiastic agreement for visiting the grounds of nearby Valley Forge Park. He brought a blanket and some bottles of water along, and they stopped along the way to pick up some deli sandwiches and two apples. The air was warm and clear as they laughed together, stretched out on the blanket on the picturesque grounds, enjoying their turkey sandwiches and fruit dessert. Tyler had not known in advance that Alyssa somehow had managed to sneak along a bottle of Napa Valley Cabernet Sauvignon, and of course a corkscrew opener. By four o'clock all had gone beautifully. They kissed with fervor, hugged each other tightly, smiling, laughing in the warm sunshine.

Then it began. "Ya know Ty. I was reading the other day about all the Russian interference in recent elections in Texas. Seems that some old conservatives there are still trying to get that crazy state to secede from the Union. The Russian government would love to see more dissent in our democratic system, and you know your parents are over there, and…"

"Wait, wait. You bring this stuff up now? Where are you reading that crap?"

"It's not 'stuff', not 'crap'. It's been all over Facebook, Twitter, Google. Don't you read the news?"

"Yes, Alyssa, I read the news," Tyler quickly and firmly responded, his facial demeanor now turning to what can best be described as anger. After all, it had been a perfect afternoon until now. *Why does she do this,* his mind racing. "I read lots of news, from definitely more sources than you. Those social media giants years ago used to be called before a more balanced Congress on many occasions and quizzed on end about the deliberate misinformation they were putting out. They were in with the elites and the globalists. They knew their business was worldwide and could care less about traditional American conservative values. They spread conspiracy theories to weaken individualism. Do you believe everything you read on the internet? Used to be twenty-five percent false, made up, now way over fifty percent, and let me tell you…"

Alyssa's turn to interrupt, raising her voice. "Tyler, my poor outcast. Stop! You get all that nonsense not from the news, but from your cousin Alex, your parents, your grandparents, even that old great-grandfather you have over there in Siberia, the one you call 'Papa Bear.'" She paused, realizing now that maybe she had gone too far. She had attacked his family whom she knew he missed. He realized it too. Sitting up on the blanket, he put his head down, his hands folded over his knees. Quiet. Arguing with her now was futile. What to do?

She sensed his moment of increasing despair. This had been too beautiful a day with this wonderful guy. The late afternoon sun still felt warm. Why ruin it? *Not now, but someday, I'll convince him.* She reached out from behind him and placed both her arms around his shoulders, her face close to his ear, hugging him. "I'm sorry, I'm sorry, I shouldn't have..." She smartly decided to turn quiet.

——— ★ ———

*"It's better to offer no excuse than a bad one."*
George Washington

# CHAPTER 9

★

## CLIMATE CHANGE

Some forty years ago when it all started, it was called "global warming." Well, that was found to be too alarming as heat forecasts did not pan out, so the tag changed to "climate change." The problem with that new tag was that the climate alarmists had indoctrinated from billionaire non-scientists to young school children to teenagers and millennials, that man's activities, especially the burning of fossil fuels emitting the greenhouse gas carbon dioxide, were warming our atmosphere leading to dozens of adverse impacts, so therefore we had to eliminate fossil fuels and **save the planet**. We had to keep the climate basically the same, or disaster! The contributing scientists to the universal acceptance of the continuing United Nations pronouncements that man was overwhelmingly responsible for the warming, say with ninety to ninety-five percent assurance, convinced the many that this position was the truth. Hurricanes, floods, and fires would increase in ferocity and number, seas would rise overwhelming island civilizations and coastal communities, glaciers would melt wiping out many of man's water supplies, the oceans would become more acidic and harm marine life.

So widespread this doctrine had become that it was left to California and subsequently the United States to lead the way to salvation. Forgotten was the history of the sun and the ever-changing earth, both already halfway through their life cycles. That the climate on earth had always been changing, ice ages and melting, warming and cooling, that the Sahara desert had been a grassland only a few thousand years ago, that New Jersey had been solidly under ice only fifteen thousand years ago, that "warmest on record" really meant since official temperature records began about 1880 on a planet four and a half billion years old, that some climate scientists who believed that the greenhouse gas culprit carbon dioxide (that compound we mammals breath out with each breath) had a diminishing effect on the current warming period but were silenced, that there were so many other warming/cooling variants like the sun's nuclear variables, the annual changing of warm/cool ocean currents, the wild flow of the earth's jet streams – all ignored. Some idealists believed if man even had some, even a small, impact on our climate, then rules, laws, regulations, and technology had to move ahead to achieve a pure green agenda. The sooner the better. No "pollution" of any kind. Carbon neutral. It was the truth we were told.

The science had been 'done.' Remember former Vice President Al Gore in a speech delivered some thirty years ago said something to the effect: "We are on a fast moving train and about to go off the cliff." And some thirteen years ago, around 2021, one of the very richest men in the world published a dramatic book on his solutions to preventing a climate disaster, a climate catastrophe. Some scientists stated it did not matter what man did to drastically reduce carbon dioxide emissions short term as there was so much of a recent increase up in the atmosphere already that such steps would only benefit man in the next century, meaning short-term doom, long -term survival if only the 'right' actions moved forward immediately – eliminate the human emissions of CO2.

Now yes, Tyler was getting all this "information" from his relatives in Vladivostok, not from any current source at Penn or in the U.S. or from the worldwide web. So, he decided to find his own answers. He had just received a letter from his grandfather referring to the slight warming of the lower Siberian permafrost and the valuable minerals the American geologists were recovering. He remembered he had learned from his physics teacher in high school who kept repeating to his students that "science is never done, never settled." New observations steadily disprove older ones in every field of science. Tyler learned that scientific theories and then hypotheses must be constantly under challenge and review. Only constant repetition of observation proves a scientific law, like the acceptance of the law of gravity. Tyler wondered whether that high school teacher was now censored.

After reading his grandfather's letter two more times, he set himself upon a new goal – to learn as much as he could about this once controversial subject now cast in stone. The week following his good time, bad time, good time with Alyssa, he set himself upon the goal of two hours in the Penn library each afternoon after his final class of the day. He would seek to find every journal and book on the subject and guess whether or not the library had been "cleansed." To his great surprise and delight, it had not been – yet. Here were references to magazine articles, pamphlets, and books taking positions on all sides of the global warming, climate change story. He dug in.

Two weeks later, he just had to see Professor Evans again and reveal his findings. He was so excited about his new knowledge. Sunday evening. That would be a good time to visit the Prof at his apartment. Things would be slow and calm, ideal for intellectual discussion. His knock on the door was answered right away. "Who is it?" Dr. Evans' tone sounded grouse, like he didn't wish to be disturbed.

"Tyler, sir. Is this a bad time?" No answer back but in a moment the door opened slowly. The Prof looked tired, stern, but he opened the door fully, beckoning Tyler in with a head nod.

"Nah, I think I just had two much wine with my little dinner and I was about to take a short nap... You are always welcome, my boy. Not too many I can talk with these days. So, what's on your mind now?" perking up a bit. It was energizing for him to converse with a student who was out of the indoctrinated mold, and certainly for him to intellectually engage with another professor or assistant professor was not in the cards anymore.

"I know this is not your field, sir, but I thought you might have some background on ... uh ... global warming," Tyler answered hesitantly.

The Prof's opening sternness turned into a big grin. "Ho, ho, ah yes, come in, come in. Sit down here, pointing towards the living room couch. Love the subject. I used to talk with my friends, the climatologists. Yes, global warming. Such alarm, and then when the fast temperature rises predicted by their models were not happening, they changed the name to climate change. Then they brainwashed everyone that man's emissions of carbon dioxide nevertheless would eventually destroy the planet. Disaster, catastrophe! My God, the planet's climate has always been changing and will continue to always change. Don't they know every few thousand years the earth changes its degree of tilt just as we tilt annually for winter and summer, that it goes around the sun not in a circle but an elliptical path, that it wobbles like a top, that we are traveling through space at 67,000 miles per hour churning our atmosphere and ocean currents." My gosh, boy, oh sorry ... I forgot. You're here for what?"

Tyler's face lit up with amazement. How would a professor of English literature know anything too much about climate change? "Well, you got the ball rolling, but I just wanted to see if you had any simple background on a subject I have been researching. It seems you know more than a little and ..."

"And what?" The Prof chuckled heartily out loud. "You think I don't know about the devastating New York hurricane of 1893 with its waist high flooding in Brooklyn, the many houses destroyed, the uprooting of 100 big trees in Central Park? And then the recent doomsdays talk about man induced climate change producing more hurricanes and bad weather events? Ha! But young man, as a student you are not permitted to be skeptical, yet... I got off track. You are here to discuss what, specifically that is."

"Okay, got it," Tyler said. "You have thought about all this. You do have a background. You bring up another side. But the facts seem to say that over the last 150 years, since we started burning fossil fuels at the start of the Industrial Revolution, that its emission, carbon dioxide, is a greenhouse gas, very small concentration in the atmosphere and nowhere close to the largest greenhouse gas, water vapor, but nevertheless its increase is enough to raise the worldwide average temperature and therefore result in what the scientists call 'adverse impacts'. All these scientists have reached a major consensus on this. Our country is now in a desperate scramble to get off fossil fuel burning as fast as possible. We have alternates, called going green, like our elimination of the coal industry, next off oil and gas, the big increase in wind farms and solar panels and biofuels to produce electricity. It's creating a lot of new jobs just as we lose jobs in the old energy sector. The adjustment is being made. The impacts have been well documented. While it has not been dramatic, the temperatures have continued to rise. Sea levels are rising, glaciers are melting, and even my family in Siberia fully know it's happening. The Russian Siberian permafrost has melted enough to recover buried minerals. The United States is leading the way to a clean planet.

"But sir, what I am learning most from my research is that the planet is not in jeopardy. The old books and magazines are full of stories of past environmental tragedies that we have recovered from. That man's invention of air conditioning that allowed Singapore, Florida, Atlanta to prosper and boom is just one example of man's ability to adapt to a warming climate. That not mentioned in today's literature is the beneficial impacts on northern areas, Russia, Canada, like more food production, wheat. Even here and in New England, Minneapolis, people are enjoying a shorter winter..."

"Well, you mean there are two sides to the story?" Professor Evans chuckled briefly then put on a more serious face. "And you learned how all this came about? The push by a very few influential persons on the United Nations to create a huge panel of scientists, many of which were not grounded in climate science, the publications by their well funded elite scientific group on the quote "policymakers" of the so called quote "consensus" that man's increasing $CO_2$ emissions were responsible for the observed increase in average world wide temperatures, and that without fast responsible reductions so many adverse impacts lay ahead. That a university scientist near here published his famous hockey stick graph showing how fast temperatures would rise with just a little more $CO_2$ concentration in the atmosphere. Of course, that hasn't happened. That in Washington, our non-scientific Supreme Court judges ruled in a five to four vote that if the EPA found carbon dioxide emissions endangering public welfare, then it could be regulated as a quote "pollutant." And you know Tyler, that senior science group at the UN never reported to the policymakers all the caveats, warnings, and uncertainties in the underlying reports. Yet many powerful politicians and billionaires and liberal journalists bought their summary political story..." The dimly lit room became quiet, like neither one knew what to say next. Tyler squirmed in his seat as the professor dropped his shoulders and appeared glum.

"Sir, I should go now. Whatever is happening out there, I see so much scientific and engineering progress here and in Europe but like it's nowhere else. Did the U.S. got hoodwinked? How can I really know what is responsible for this slow but steady warming period? Or how long it will last and to what extent. Is man ten percent responsible, twenty-five percent, fifty percent, seventy-five percent, ninety percent? Who really knows?

"I read where the sun's simple hydrogen atom makes up of just one proton and one electron falls into the density of the core and with atomic fusion turns into the next element up, helium, and in that simple process, all the atomic energy from this reaction is released out towards us, but it's occurring at varying rates. So how much of our climate change is just natural variability? Who really knows? We do have turmoil going on in our country over these mandatory job changes. The fossil fuel layoffs here are far exceeding the new green jobs. This so called change to a 'green economy' seems to be in turmoil. I believe the planet's in an economic mess, but that we will survive ever changing climate conditions, no matter which way they go. Professor Evans, aren't we smart enough to adapt, to invent, to mitigate, to prepare for whatever comes?"

"Surely, my boy," the Prof said with a slight smile, "but don't tell anyone for fear these days of getting yourself mentally punished by the 'know it all's', that such progress you describe could really be achieved much more rationally. Look, as we are steadily destroying our petroleum industry here, has anyone thought about the thousands of products made from petroleum derivatives like plastics, clothing, health products and so on and so on? So, what is happening in our craze is Brazil and

Mexico with their huge offshore reserves and the Middle East with their vast reserves are booming. And we see China and India with nearly half the world's population continuing to put more carbon dioxide into the air with their inexpensive coal burning, a resource in supply for another 400 years." The professor rested his case and raised the palm of his hand towards Tyler as if to say 'go in peace.w

★

*Believe half of what you see and none of what you hear.*
Ben Franklin

# CHAPTER 10

★

## VIOLENCE = ENTERTAINMENT

"Come on Tyler, you used to watch these flicks with us on Saturday nights. Now you just want to go see your girlfriend, Alyssa." The guys had played three hours of tag football that afternoon, had enjoyed a few beers and some cheeseburgers at the local pub, and now had gathered at an apartment a short ways down the block from Tyler's. Yes, Ty felt tired and relaxed, but friend John was no longer at these events, and he knew very shortly the guys would break out the marijuana and the party atmosphere would heighten. But that super levity was not the factor bothering Tyler. It was the fact the guys would play one violent movie after another on the big screen TV.

"Well, you turkeys, if any of you had girlfriends as good looking as Alyssa, you would bug out at eight o'clock too," Tyler boldly offered with a grin. They laughed in unison and didn't offer any other response. He walked slowly towards his apartment knowing he had plenty of time to shower and change before Alyssa would come over. But his slow walk was really because he wanted to sort out in his mind what was really going on in the field of entertainment. He had read that over the last fifty years some seventy percent of movie labels carried the V label, V for violent content. *So, people are entertained by violent scenes,* he mused. Must be part of human nature, he thought. Man has been readily and steadily violent since the dawn of homo sapiens. With the advent of civilizations, weapons were created and steadily improved. and the violence among men just became more gruesome. He remembered reading some seventy million people were killed during World War II. No wars like that since but lots of little wars, and even in non-war years some 500,000 killings a year take place around the world. He had read that in some obscure magazine.

Further, he had heard that even though guns are now banned in the United States, there are some 400 million guns out there, more that the American population number. And some 200 mass shootings just in the United States since the mid 1990's. So those few people still going to church keep saying we have to **pray** for peace. The press people and politicians keep saying we have to **hope** for peace. And the Hollywood people keep saying we all just have to **love** each other, but then they go right back to their studios and make another violent movie. Then he remembered his high school biology class where he learned that from our early survival genetics, we have the dual capacities to be both competitive and altruistic. We can be violent when we have to be, or we can be cooperative when it's to our advantage. So, despite all the rules to keep us orderly, there are times we can go off the deep end. How in the world can we resolve unending natural conflict without resorting to violent behavior? Tyler's racing mind suddenly stopped when he arrived at his apartment house. Alyssa was there, standing erect, arms crossed.

"I knocked, I called your cell, where have you been? It's way after nine." She did not look pleased.

"Oh my gosh, I didn't realize it got so late. I was thinking, I..." he hesitated. Alyssa face could only be described as looking mad.

"I'm sorry. I got caught up in something. Hey," he brightened. "My treat. Let's go up. I'll change fast. I'll do anything, take you anywhere you want, you name it."

Alyssa relented, dropping her arms, extending a quizzical but not an unpleasant look towards Tyler. *Well, he's so damn good looking, and that great masculine voice.*

★

*Hope, prayers, love = Peace?*
The Storyteller

# CHAPTER 11

★

## GUARANTEED INCOME

The question came up in Alyssa's Political Science class the Monday after Tyler had to make up for his Saturday's meanderings to her, showering her with her favorite ice cream treat at a nearby eatery, then her favorite red wine back at his apartment, lights down, good music on, and his best romantic behavior. Their togetherness did not always have to end in controversy.

"Professor Schwartz, can I ask a question before this class ends?" a scholarly looking but baby faced young man asked. The professor scowled slightly as he obviously did not like to receive many questions from students. They might have too much to say as he often noted. "Go ahead, we have five minutes left," he replied dourly.

"Over the weekend, I was back home, and my grandfather and father were arguing about our guaranteed income. My grandfather was saying it was really unnecessary that such a benefit was ever passed by Congress. In the old days, people had to have an incentive to work, to be productive, and they were paid based upon their merit. That. actually, if you consider all the benefits already paid to the middle classes and lower economic classes along with their lower taxes, we have already achieved a great amount of economic equality. He said the program was costing way too much, that taxes on productive businesses had to be raised to help pay for it, and still the government runs a huge deficit in its spending. And worse, so many idle people just take the money along with all the other welfare benefits and just become too lazy in trying to improve their lot…"

"Get to your question. You're droning."

"Oh, okay … but my father said it was passed in order to give the lower classes of people some basic security. You know, free from want, a good thing, but then he said it was a huge political fight to get it passed. Almost everybody gets it. So, my question is, what was the politics in getting this thing done, and is it working?" The young man's eyes behind his dark rimmed glasses were wide open, as was his mouth. He almost looked frightened as he waited for Professor Schwartz to respond.

The professor tightened his lips, stood up tall from his chair behind his desk, moved to the front, and began to speak with a tone of great authority. "Students, let's make this clear. As I have been patiently trying to teach you, politics in a democracy is always about the art of achieving the practical. It takes into account different and opposing viewpoints on how we achieve our agreements. Sure, there were arguments in passing the Guaranteed Annual Income legislation, but they were about how to do it, its shape, size, and form, not whether or not it was needed. Even the Pope in Rome, whom not many people listen to anymore, has stated most of the world's people live in a sad state of daily insecurity. And now that our public corporations work for all stakeholders not just their shareholders, the wealth our nation creates is to be shared by all. So, after all the debate, it was decided by the majority that the income would be paid $1,000 monthly, per person. The family maximum would be $5,000 paid monthly, adding up to $12,000 to $60,000 a year. But, of course, the benefits would start being reduced for anyone earning a taxable income over $100,000 so that the top twenty-five of the earning population would see little or no benefit. So, class, the legislation has been a tremendous success in reducing the air of financial insecurity that so many of our citizens were feeling. We proved that adding to income does not result in a disincentive to work. Yes, a great success for our nation," the professor proudly stated, exhibiting a very rare slight smile.

There was a short pause in the classroom conversation. Alyssa sat back in her chair, expressing a look of comfort on her face. But another student than the one who first asked the question spoke out. "Sir, was there any initial debate on whether there would be any detrimental impacts of passing such a guaranteed income for well over half our population?"

Professor Schwartz was taken back. He stiffened up and raised his voice. "Of course not. Don't you know where you are, son? This is progressive America. We are creating equality, equity, security, and yes, we are creating happiness, and I already just told you, no matter what else you might hear, guaranteed income is not a disincentive to work. Class is over. Dismissed!"

That evening Alyssa was alone in her dorm room and sat back on her bed thinking, thinking, thinking. She was pondering the last words of Professor Evans about the word 'happiness.' *What is it that creates happiness? In a society at large. In a group? In a couple? In an individual?* She thought long and hard but could not come up with a single phrase for all. Maybe harmony among family and friends, maybe a feeling of unexplainable contentment, maybe physical security, maybe financial security, maybe self-fulfillment, but hey, maybe **freedom**, freedom to follow one's ambitions, to achieve, to accomplish something meaningful. *I think I have all of that. I've come a long way from freshman year when I didn't know anything. I think I'm committed now. It's only those contested moments with Ty that...* She too had difficulty sleeping that night.

★

The bluebird said to the robin:
*I'm so happy to be free as a bird.*

# CHAPTER 12

★

# IMMIGRATION

Ricardo was a full-time student, in his senior year at Penn. He was on a full-time tuition free scholarship as an 'included minority' in the school's 'diversification' program. For extra dollars in order to have a little spending money, he worked fifteen hours a week at the university's Student Health Clinic. His major was Sociology, and his goal was to become a social worker helping the medical community rehabilitate drug users. He understood there was a serious shortage of qualified people in that demanding field. He also understood the majority of Americans did not overuse and have drug problems, but that the numbers who did kept climbing dramatically over the last ten years.

One thing really did bother him though. Every student entering the clinic had to identify himself or herself as White, Black, Asian, Hispanic, Other, and if they were LGBTQ. He himself of course was 'Other' and not LGBTQ. All that to him was not very meaningful. Why couldn't everyone just indicate American or country of Citizenship? What was wrong with *assimilation*, he thought to himself, since that was what he strived for himself and the way he wanted to treat everyone else. Ricardo was born in Mexico. His mother was a fairly dark skinned Mexican, maybe part Spanish, part native Mayan perhaps. His father was a white European German, but his father's mother was a Black

African. His father's brother was considered 'colored' and felt very uncomfortable in Germany. Ricardo's complexion was somewhere in the middle of that mix, but really he was quite good looking with his slightly tanned face.

When Ricardo was five years old, his father was killed in a car accident and his mother learned he had just taken a huge loan on a new business venture. As she could not repay the loan and the family finances dwindled to almost nothing, she found a middleman who for $5,000 could smuggle her and her young son into the United States where her cousin lived. Growing up in Arizona, Ricardo became a new American citizen under a special program to take care of such children.

In the final analysis, he just chuckled to himself every time a new student patient entered the clinic and Ricardo had to see that all the forms were filled in. Thinking back, however, he recounted stories of the thousands and thousands of so called "illegals" who each month for the last fifty years had crossed that border, putting themselves ahead of all those who waited for legal immigration. The number had increased the last ten years, but there were no longer outcries of stopping the flow due to the fact their numbers were an increasing burden on welfare programs that had been originally established only for Americans. Dissent with the government was not legally for-bidden but simply not printed nor on any other type of news service. The secret word out was that the one party govern-ment saw all those immigrants as future votes in a government still calling itself a democracy.

On a Saturday morning full of heavy rain showers and hence no flag football that day, Tyler took himself to the Student Health Clinic to visit his friend John. He had learned that John was being treated there for his drug addiction problem, and Tyler was hopeful all would work out so that John could get back on his feet and graduate the end of May. After waiting in the clinic's lobby for several minutes, Tyler was greeted by Ricardo. "Hello, the receptionist told me you wanted to see John Frazier? Is that right?" Ricardo said to Tyler rising from his lobby chair.

"Yes, a very good friend of mine. Can I see him? Is he improving?"

Ricardo looked stunned. It appeared he did not know how to answer. Tyler squinted his eyes, searching for a response.

The answer finally came. "Yes, your friend John was here quite a bit the last month, but we couldn't help him. Haven't you heard?" Again, a long pause.

Tyler took a deep breath before responding. "No, no, I haven't heard anything since I saw him a couple of weeks ago and he told me he was getting help, and that finally he was going to lick this thing. That's why I came. He wasn't answering his phone. So, what's going on?" His face now lit up with concern.

Ricardo slowly replied, deliberate in tone of voice but softly, "Well, the staff here couldn't keep him on the withdrawal protocols ... so he was sent to the hospital when he really became uncontrollable, and ... the other day, expecting him back here ... we were told he died in the hospital. He had somehow smuggled something in and overdosed. I think fentanyl. So sorry..."

Tyler was speechless. His mouth dropped open, and he just stared at Ricardo's face, which was now looking straight down. Both looked troubled.

*In grief, there are no words.*

# CHAPTER 13

★

# WORLD DISORDER

Alyssa was feeling so exhilarated after another Monday's Political Science class she couldn't wait to see Tyler. *I really love this guy, maybe he will come around in his backward thinking.* She knew he would be in the library late Monday afternoon, so she began her search shortly before dinnertime. There he was, a book wide open on the table, with two others adjacent. The large library room was so big and quiet that she scribbled a note, slowly approached him, and without a word dropped the note on his open book. He looked up in surprise and then down at the note. It read "Can we meet for dinner at 6 in the Houston cafeteria? Shake your head yes or no." After his initial look of surprise, he nodded to her in the affirmative. She smiled and walked away briskly, without a spoken word.

The chicken pot pie and the mixed salad they both had selected weren't too bad. Jello for dessert. Their conversation had been muted, mostly about whether any good streaming movies were coming out. "You seem rather content over there, Miss Alyssa. Are you having a good day?" Tyler quizzed, looking relaxed. He loved jello.

"Yes, I am," she quickly answered. "And I wanted to discuss with you a subject I think we can finally agree on. World affairs. I've been doing a lot of reading, also talking with my Dad a lot. You remember he was in the Army and saw duty in Afghanistan. And I know you told me once you were afraid that small weapons of mass destruction were no longer out of the question. That it could be a small rogue nation or even a wealthy terrorist group that could develop biological, chemical, or even atomic weapons. And I have learned that the world of nations, and certainly not the United Nations, seem incapable of getting to stop such a threat, and while there have been no major wars for a long time, there are little wars of some type, it seems everywhere. And everyone is trying to arm to their teeth as they say, and..."

"Whoa... Alyssa! You are on a tear here. What's up? Why are you on this subject all of a sudden?"

A pause, her face looking serious. "Because I know you follow world affairs, and I am so concerned. We certainly do not see eye to eye on our transformation of America, but we still need world order, world peace. I want your insights."

Tyler felt important all of a sudden. "Okay, okay, where do we start? You mentioned your dad in Afghanistan. As soon as we pulled out the Taliban took over again. Women are back to second rate, no education, no big jobs. Everybody follows the strict Sharia rules. That sure was a predictable outcome. We just have to hope our aerial surveillance is picking up any terrorists' training camps. So go around the world – the Middle East still an ongoing mess. The Shiites and the Sunnis, forever antagonists in the Islam religion, have yet to reconcile like the Christian Catholics and Protestants did long ago. Syria has yet to settle its long civil war. Iraq is a puppet of strong-armed Iran. The Iranians now have atomic bombs and missiles despite the attempts to dissuade them with weak treaties. China boosted their economy by buying oil from them. Israel keeps its military up to full speed to discourage any attacks on it. A second state, that of Palestine is still always in the talking stage and it's still dominated by Iranian supported terrorists. Over to

Africa, still thirty nations dominated by corrupt governments. Little progress.

"Europe, weak economically with slow growth or no growth economies, weak militarily as NATO underfinanced again and Germany beholden to Russia. Back across the ocean: South America, some struggling democracies with some slow economic growth and still some socialist dictatorships like Venezuela and Cuba with suffering masses. Up to Canada, not too bad – smart population taking care of each other with still a lot of freedom. Same back across the ocean with bright spots in Australia and New Zealand – strong democracies with a love of freedom and controls over too much socialism. Up to Japan – smart, hard-working people but overshadowed, and like Korea subservient to the now dominant China..."

"Ty! You are going so fast. But go ahead, China. What about China?" Alyssa interrupted.

"What can I say? China is number one. The largest military in the world, now with nuclear submarines and aircraft carriers. They could finally take their long sought after prize, Taiwan, anytime they wanted, but they hesitate because of the advanced technology that Taiwan brings to the mainland. China now controls the shipping in the South China Sea. They have invested heavily across the Middle East and Africa, and those nations curtsy to them in return. And, of course, China has now surpassed the U.S. economy as the number one in Gross National Product. And we are now subservient to them. The Communists have beaten your Progressives."

"Now wait. That is not what we are to talk about. Let's stick with overseas," Alyssa tightened up her composure but tried not to look annoyed at Tyler's last comment.

"Look, I'm no genius, love bud. I had a course in World History last semester, and I talk with my parents, grandparents, and even my great grandfather about world events, but

I don't know it all. Just what is it you want to know? What are you after?"

"Ty, look. It's simple. I want world peace. I want your ideas on where we're going. And if there's world disorder, how can we straighten it out?"

"Alyssa, my darling Alyssa. Listen, babe, we have covered this subject before. The world's major religions were basically founded over a short period of time because man is by nature disorderly. We have ongoing conflict as part of our human nature. No two brains are alike. We are all different. You know that. You want to resolve conflict without violence. So do I, but let's face reality. Conflict is a natural human condition. And you also want everyone to be happy. Like Denmark, Allysa?

"Yes, let's take Denmark," Tyler pursued. "Ten years ago, the polls said the Danish were the happiest people in the world."

"Yes, I know. You're right. I have been thinking a lot about happiness lately. Let's talk," she said with alacrity.

"Okay," Tyler quickly responded. "Have to go back to the Second World War. The Nazi's were quite cruel, and starvation in Europe was rampant. Denmark escaped the worst of it but witnessed what its neighbors were going through. After the war, a lot of the European monarchies lost their power positions and government reforms were introduced which would provide more security for the common folks, the masses. It was called the welfare state, or Social Democracy, or cradle to the grave security. Now remember the Danes are a rather homogeneous society and only about five million people. We covered all this in our Sociology classes, remember? Their population is not very diverse, so like-minded people tend to help each other more. They have a strong sense of community and helping each other. They have a highly educated population, health care for everyone. No need for a big military budget. But they do pay for all that welfare. The average family is paying some forty-five percent in income taxes plus a high national sales tax, twenty-five percent. They don't have big minority class problems, nor do they have big natural disasters that can cause so much misery and money. They have some big industries that supply jobs. And importantly they still have a measure of personal freedom. The government isn't telling them what to say or do, like here. Very, very different than our diverse United States with a past tradition of rugged individualism, natural disasters like floods, fires, droughts, hurricanes. We are an immigrant society of all kinds." He paused to take a breath.

"Tyler, man, how do you know so much?" Alyssa said in good humor. "But now we have that sense of common community, that welfare state you call it, but one that protects everyone equally from basic want. Are we not now the happiest nation in the world?" She half giggled, not sure herself of the answer.

"Ha, ha, ha," he responded without the slightest hint of a smile. "Very funny, sweetheart. You are a dreamer. Why do you think some twenty million of us have escaped this nightmare and gone to Siberia? Look, I have no problem with our big heart. As a country built with immigrants, even our indigenous probably migrated in from Asia across the straits of Alaska thousands of years ago. People from around the world still want to come here for our advantages. A big welfare system, the second largest economy in the world, the absence of cruel dictatorial regimes. But should they not come in orderly? Legally?"

"We're not talking about immigration, Ty. We are talking about the world a mess. Just a few exceptions where there is no war, no big corrupt government, no cruel dictator. Yes, Denmark an exception to the world disorder, and I guess the other Scandinavian states, and Switzerland and New Zealand, and…

"Yes, Alyssa, and go on … when you know there are 200 nations out there. You mention only a few. So, we agree, most of the world is in disorder, despite the United Nations' endless meetings where people are half polite to each other and to themselves laughing in mockery."

She replied. "So, we have over 300 million of us here, and now some chasing their crazy dreams in Siberia, but we can be happy as a nation here and either withdraw into our social democracy or try to bring about positive change to the world." Alyssa threw out the challenge to Tyler.

"A choice?" he responded. "Live in our own social mess or exert ourselves overseas tying to straighten out all those other messes? The biggest problem I have now come to learn is that here in this America is the lack of freedom. How do I succeed in life unless I become a worker with low pay and big benefits, or a worker in a boring job, or learn computer science and work for one of the big prosperous globalist companies with a market potential of seven billion people? That's not happiness. Or do I join the Army or Foreign Service and keep trying with futility to bring peace and honesty to all those disturbed countries... Come on Alyssa, tell me how happy you are going to be with your life trying to change the bad behavior of those other countries or staying here in your social work trying to successfully change maybe one in ten of those out there with demons in their heads?" Tyler retreated back in his chair, thinking now perhaps he was going too far with her.

"Well maybe that one in ten I rescue will be a very noble and honorable thing. Maybe I'll be happy with that," she answered somewhat sarcastically.

Half the lights in the cafeteria suddenly went off. They were the only ones left. They had gotten nowhere.

★

*What a wonderful world.* Louie Armstrong

# CHAPTER 14

★

# IMPERIAL CHINA

Tyler continued his library searches. Now the subject of China. He thought of "imperial" as anything thought to be long gone. It had referred to powerful nations that had expanded beyond their borders and had become empires. The end of European colonies in Africa, the independence of several nations once under British rule, the disintegration of the Union of Soviet Socialist Republics are all recent examples pointing to the end of empires. But now the once isolated nation of China, as the writer Rudyard Kipling perhaps once stated "There lies a sleeping giant; best let her sleep," or Napoleon Bonaparte who perhaps said, "China is a sleeping giant. Let her lie and sleep, for when she awakens, she will shake the world." By the year 2000 China had fully awakened.

Admitted to the World Trade Organization in 2001, its cheap labor was producing and exporting billions of dollars of inexpensive goods around the world. The lower and middle classes in America were awash in less expensive goods than American producers could manufacture. The industrious Asian nation even had become the world's largest steel producer. China loosened its dominant control over a host of industries and in certain areas allowed foreign investment and state controlled capitalism. Of a population of a billion three, hundreds of millions of Chinese were now benefiting from the nation's new jobs and huge trade surplus. But some economic free-doms did not mean political freedoms. The Communist Party kept a tight lid on political dissent and protests. While perhaps an internal political nightmare, both internally and externally the nation boomed economically. Infrastructure projects like high-speed trains, bridges, roads, city skyscrapers all mush-roomed while investment projects around the world accel-erated. Three keys were important in this remarkable rate of growth. One was strict control over the foreign investors who had been developing the nation's manufacturing base; a second was the squelching of any dissent from the wide number of international companies eyeing the huge China market; and the third was the insidious 'stealing' of foreign technology. All the while the nation was substantially building upon its military capabilities. By 2033, China had the world's largest economy, become the biggest manufacturer, and had attained the world's largest and most advanced military. Dominating. It was the new Imperial China.

*Boring, boring, boring,* Tyler said to himself as he closed the last book. He had learned all this by searching books in the library, certainly not in any classroom. *Seems nobody cares about this.* But then he rethought what he was just thinking. Maybe not so boring. Yes, the American government is asleep. We are now second rate, led around by our noses by these clever Asians, but... my family, and millions of others, fleeing to Siberia to build a new America – they are awake, they under-stand. *Sunday night. I have to go talk with Professor Evans.*

"Oh, not again, lad. Why do you come so late?" Professor Evans laughed as he answered the loud knock on his apartment door. "Only kidding, I'm still up enjoying my after dinner wine, a nice New Zealand Sauvignon Blanc, but even if I'm half asleep I enjoy chatting with you. You're a little bit unusual, you know."

"Sorry, sir, I just can't get something off my mind again, and you have a way. I mean..."

"Sure, sure, I understand," said the professor quickly. "Sorry, I said unusual, but actually there are millions of you left, even after the millions already fled to New America. It's just that you can't talk out loud... So, you come to chat with me. Me, an old outcast." He paused.

"You are not old, Professor Evans. My gosh, my grandfather and my great grandfather living in New America are older than you are. You are so wise. Why don't you go there?"

"Well," he replied. "I've thought about it, especially after they removed my tenure, but I think I'll just hang around on my pension, enjoy the wine and change of seasons, and pray every morning there will be enough Tylers coming along who can gather together and restore this nation I once loved to its former greatness. I may seem defeatist, but down deep I just don't want to give up."

"Never thought that way, sir," Tyler said lighting up. "Think I told you this already. I have a goal of marrying my dream girl after graduation and taking the two of us to New America. I just never thought there is any hope here. Do you think we have a chance?"

The two stared at each other for several moments, in complete silence. The light from the two table lamps barely showing their solemn faces. "Maybe there is a chance, sir," Tyler finally continued. "But how do we overcome China? They are now so dominant. Even if we change our politics, even if we restore debate and openness and new ideas, even if we restore our old entrepreneurial spirit. They are so far ahead of us now."

The professor took a long stare at Tyler. "Perhaps you're right, my boy. I shouldn't get optimistic just out of nowhere, now, should I?" He now suddenly looked depressed Tyler thought, and Ty cringed his jaw in regret – maybe he should let his wise new friend believe in hope, hope America can be restored. But the prof continued on. "Facts are facts. The reality is our government is so far in debt. And now with uncontrolled welfare spending, you know, everyone is taken care of for every need, and with the rise in interest rates eating up the revenues from our higher tax rates and the new taxes, we've had to turn to rich China to buy our excessive debt. If we had just printed money to cover it, we would have massive inflation. You know, from everything I have read our economists are so confused over all this, but the ones in our one party now run the show. Spend, spend, spend. Even so, they can't seem to agree on anything about the future from all this deficit spending, so we are so inconsistent and things get worse. In China you don't hear about any disagreements. Whatever the Party wants, they do. No dissent. So far, they're winning."

The professor's insights encouraged Tyler to go on. "I'm afraid I have to come to the same conclusion, sir. All my research points to that. Their economy has grown the last thirty years far faster than our sluggish growth. They have had massive foreign investment pouring into their country from nations all over the world. International companies find their own growth spurts in their huge economy. They made it a point to lend to developing countries so then they can influence them economically, politically, and culturally as well. They migrated from making cheap products with cheap labor to becoming a manufacturing powerhouse. Their stolen technology led to developing advanced technology on their own." Again, another long pause.

"So, I leave you, young Mr. Tyler with the thought that all this is beyond economics. They are a smart race. They work hard. They have been a nation for a couple thousand years. They have their traditional cultures, very different than ours.

They did not Westernize. They dominate the world in their own unique manner."

It was time to end this despair. With head bowed, Tyler rose and bid his "Goodnight sir. We'll talk again."

——— ★ ———

*To learn who rules over you, simply find out*
*whom you are not allowed to criticize.*
Perhaps Voltaire

# CHAPTER 15

★

## THE LOVE OF GAMBLING

"Hey, Ty, Spring break coming up!" Alyssa shouted out with a smile. "Come on now babe, you have to get your mind off of John for a while and have a good time." The two were holding hands, walking slowly on a warm Spring evening towards Tyler's apartment after a quiet Saturday dinner at a restaurant across the river from the Penn campus. Their conversation had been pleasant and somewhat restrained until she broke out with that remark. His mind had been on some neat music, soft lights, and an intense make out scene on his couch or even into his bedroom. "You know, my parents are up to sending us to Las Vegas for a few days. Of course, Fort Lauderdale now has gambling too and a wild beach scene, or if all that is too far, we could go to Atlantic City. It's been booming there the last few years with all the casinos." She turned and looked into his eyes for an answer as they continued walking.

"Hold on. Now what's your interest in gambling all of a sudden? We have never talked about that before," Tyler asked, looking puzzled.

"Well, we never talked about it because I thought you were an old fogey on this subject. You never seemed interested in good luck, bad luck, or the thrill of winning." Her voice rose and she sounded somewhat stern with that comment.

"Now wait a minute, my princess of excitement. That's just not true. I just never appreciated this great rise in gambling throughout our society because of so many people becoming addicted to it, the fact that much more is lost than is won, that so many people lose interest in working for money and think they can get by or even get rich with all these schemes that are now everywhere. Geez!" He almost screamed dropping her hand from his. "This is your Great Society?" he quizzed her and then went silent.

"Well, on this subject maybe I'm half with you," she said. "My grandmother sort of got hooked. A gambling addict they called her. She ended up losing a lot of their family savings... you know a lot of fun as I said, but sometimes... sometimes difficult. I remember my grandfather telling me it just used to be going to Las Vegas, then Atlantic City opened big casinos, then all the computer games went online, then sports betting became legal. Then lots of other cities opened gambling casinos. It spread everywhere. Your internet email is full of gambling schemes. Governments claimed it produced a lot of income the states could use for the elderly. Never checked to see if that was the result." Her prior look of glee turned a bit sour.

"Think you answered your first question, kid," Tyler spoke up. "So, let's just forget where your parents of all people want to send us. Let's just rent a car and drive South and enjoy the Springtime wherever we find it. Just you and me. That's where I'll spend my money and not lose. I'm gambling on my making you happy."

Alyssa looked up at him and broke into a warm smile, putting her hands out towards him. "I'm in," she responded softly.

Their trip together went fine, the first three days and nights. They drove through the Virginia countryside, visited Jefferson's home at Monticello, toured the beautiful campuses of Duke and University of North Carolina, then over to the coast and the seaside resort towns of South Carolina. Finding good restaurants and good wine was all fun and exciting. No stops at the gambling casinos. It was pure ecstasy for the two in the late evenings and early mornings in their hotel beds. All the while they both avoided talk about the economy, politics, and the state of the nation.

But in the fourth evening it all came out. Both perhaps had consumed more wine than usual. That second bottle did it. The lights were dim, the table candles glowing at the resort hotel restaurant at Hilton Head. Their mutual words of admiration words went on pause, and the two simply stared into each other's eyes for what seemed like minutes. *What was this?* They both wondered. Love? Admiration? Searching? Remorse? Alyssa was the first to break the silence. "Ty, this has been so wonderful the last few days. I thought I couldn't be happier … but, you know, I just have to get this out… we've talked about after graduation we would get married, and then you want us to go join your family in Siberia, you know this New America, you call it. You say it's a wonderful place, but Ty, how can I do that? I know we don't agree on the implementation of all the things we want to do in this our country. It's not been perfect, but my commitment to my major, Sociology, I want to help. I know we are on the right track as a country. I really do want to help. How can I leave?" She finally paused. Her look at him was intense.

All the time Tyler stared into her eyes, no expression on his face, but he could feel his heart racing. *How do I answer her? What can I say?* But with her continued deep stare, her facial expression begging, he had to speak up. She continued her stare. A long pause… "Maybe I don't have the answer you're looking for. You have dated other guys. I have dated other girls. All I know is I feel something way down deep that I was meant to fall in love with you, that you are the one for me, that I can make you happy, like the last three days. Yeah, we are so much younger than so many couples that get married, but I just know I want to spend the rest of my life with you... Alyssa, can we just put this off right now? This past year we've learned so much. Two years more in school, we'll find a way."

Alyssa bowed her head down towards the table, her dessert uneaten. Tears flowed from her eyes. She couldn't look up.

———— ★ ————

*Into each life some rain must fall.*

# CHAPTER 16

★

# AN AGING MILITARY

One morning shortly after Spring break, Tyler awakened with a strange thought. The day before while walking back to his apartment he noticed passing an older looking man dressed immaculately in a military uniform. He remembered his father and grandfather briefly mentioning sometime back about America's disappointing role in several overseas conflicts, but he never had learned the history of these involvements. Not one word of these stories in any of the five classes he was now taking at Penn, not even in his American history class last year as a freshman nor the World History class he took last semester. Finishing his daily morning bathroom chores, he opened his laptop computer and quickly sent off an inquiry to Papa Bear in Russia.

That evening he had a full read on his screen. Papa Bear had wasted no time in replying. Seems that after the glory of the Second World War whereby the Allies led by the gallant United States successfully defeated Nazism in Germany, fascism in Italy and imperialism in Japan, things went downhill. After Communist North Korea invaded South Korea, the U.S. lead a successful United Nations push back, all the way to the border of China but when the Chinese military surprisingly stepped in, the world ended up with two Koreas- a closed, impoverished, Communist dictatorship to the North of the 38th parallel and a prosperous, free, democratic, capitalist South. That stalemate continues on. Then a few years later, after the Korean conflict, when the North of Vietnam pushed the French colonists out, a wider war broke out in the South with anti-government forces known as the Viet Cong along with North Korean communists' support leading the fight.

With the concept of not letting Communism with its eventual goal of world wide domination spread further, the United States stepped in with hundreds of thousands of drafted young soldiers. The draft and the rapid build up caused much anguish in the American society. It was difficult for our soldiers to know who the enemy was. North Vietnam stepped up the attack, and the Americans with poor political support decided to withdraw. It was a disaster.

Years later the radical Islamists destroyed the New York Twin Towers, prompting America to take the fight against the terrorists abroad. Stopping terrorism in the turbulent Middle East became a nightmare. The U.S. remained in Afghanistan for twenty years, futilely ending in that nation's return to the radical Muslim Taliban.

All the while the U.S. military experienced up and down cycles in weaponry, readiness and morale. After the fall of the Communist Soviet Union and the freeing of the Eastern European nations in the late 1980's, early 1990's, the military spending budget was great reduced. Then after the September 11, 2001, New York City terrorist attack, the budget was back up, at least until domestic spending pushed the military budget down again in 2009. By 2016, equipment maintenance was at a severe low and the preparedness of both America forces and the NATO forces protecting Europe were at a dismal low. But politics – Republican control 2016 to 2020 pushed the budget back up – the military was back in the saddle. Then in 2020 when political control went back to expanding the domestic social agenda, the America military became an also ran to the buildups by Russia and China. America had lost its position as the world leader, protector of freedom, and the force against evil.

Tyler scratched his head. He had a difficult time following all that Papa Bear had written, but he thought he got the main message – from its former superiority America was now a second rate military power. All that he could learn currently was that the world scene was messy, that Russia had a strong military with a massive number of atomic bombs and missiles of all ranges, access to military seaports on the Atlantic and Mediterranean and held Europe under its ominous thumb. That China had so expanded its military capabilities that it controlled the vast shipping lanes in the South China Sea and had not taken over Taiwan only because of the little island's extensive and advanced information technology prowess available to big China. He sat back and wondered what that man in the uniform he had seen passing him must be thinking now. No one at college ever mentioned military service. What to think?

★

*To be, or not to be. That is the question.*
Shakespeare's Hamlet

# CHAPTER 17

★

# THE ELITES AND THEIR COHORTS
# Ty's DILEMMA

The regular Wednesday evening and Saturday evening dates with Alyssa seemed to be on the emotional downside now with Tyler. They hugged and kissed a little, they laughed a little, and they avoided any mention of their differences. But Tyler could clearly sense the tension, the disappointment he felt with her constant glances away from his eyes, like she now wanted to avoid any type of confrontation. Their parting 'goodbyes' on each occasion were brief – a fast hug, a quick kiss on the lips, no smiles. Yet, in his mind, there was no wavering from the feeling that this girl was the one for him. No telling what was going through her mind. This constant thought in his mind seemed agonizing – *How do I get through to her? Are we on the verge of breaking up?*

Sunday night he was back tapping on the door of Professor Evans apartment, the prof not surprised at all who his visitor was at the door. "Well, come in lad. It's nice to see you again. It's been a couple of weeks."

"Well, yes, sir. We've had Spring break, and I have been to the library a lot, so..."

"So," the professor went on. "So, what brings you tonight? I am not your Wikipedia you know," he said as a matter of fact and without a smile.

"No, no sir, I know that. I just wanted your take on a couple of things," Tyler said quickly noticing the professor's mood seemed to be looking and acting, well almost depressed.

"Well, go ahead. Have a seat. I'm listening."

Tyler cleared his throat with a quick cough and began, somewhat nervously "Okay, okay, what I'm getting to is that in our move to social democracy, and you and I know how imperfect that has been, well it appears that the so called Washington 'elites' are in bed with not only the media but also the CEO's of the big international companies whose markets are the whole world not just the U.S. and also with the chiefs and workforces of the big social media companies. The cards are stacked against us!" Tyler bellowed out raising his voice. He then sat back a little waiting for a response from the grim looking professor.

"Tyler, my boy, I don't know where you get this information. Can't be from the newspapers, your cell phone news or television coverage. That's all about spreading misinformation. Your folks in Siberia? Yeah, maybe, but you know that's going to be biased the other way. Anyway, you are correct. But first, who are the 'elites' you mentioned? Aren't they not just the Washington politicians but all of those so-called journalists and the globalists plus the big brass and their bureaucratic drones running the nation?" The professor almost seemed scolding in that remark. Tyler was taken back and held his reply. "You know young man, I no longer can express a fact, let alone an opinion, about anything critical of what's going on, nor is any type of libertarian or conservative allowed to speak on our campus. So, it's difficult to find facts, truths ... I just don't know what you are going to do with yourself. You said after graduation, you wanted to marry your flame, join your family in New America. Fine do it. For me, for me here, I'll just stay, and maybe I should pray." A long silence followed.

With the professor looking down, a glum look on his face, Tyler regained his train of thought. He couldn't end this meeting on a down note. "Sir, let me not bother you with my love life. I'll continue to try to persuade her. I just wanted assurance that I was getting it straight, and I think you have confirmed it. I am getting my information from library sources that print data not just opinions. The 'elites' comprise a huge group. Their longevity with the media companies they own or that employ them, the wealth of the members of Congress and the Executive branch, their long terms in office without opposition, the executive teams of the international companies and their extravagant income, their penetration into worldwide markets with our government's support, the generous terms of employment compensation and benefits of the hundreds of thousands of government workers, the highly paid upper echelon of the hundreds of big companies that have been nationalized, the coziness of the high tech companies getting blessings and benefits from the feds for doing things as the feds direct ... so I find this, and it's true?" Tyler questioned and rested his case.

"Yes, lad, it's all very true," Professor Evans said softly still looking down. Tyler knew it was time to quietly leave.

*A lie told once remains a lie, but a lie told a thousand times becomes the truth.*

Nazi Joseph Goebbels

By late May, the school semester was ending. Tyler and Alyssa were independently making plans how to spend their summer break. They both thought without saying it out loud to one another that some short separation would be beneficial for their relationship. At this moment, they just could not seem to reconcile their lifetime ambitions. Wanting to be together was in second place right now, not by emotion but by rational thought.

"Ty, listen, I have a summer job lined up in our university hospital. Want to hear about it? Okay," she continued without a pause for his response. "It's with the Social Workers group. I'll go out with some experienced workers with those patients discharged from the hospital, to their homes, and help them get settled where there are a lot of difficulties at home. Should be super experience," she paused awaiting his response.

"That's terrific, Alyssa, right down your alley. You want so much to help people. You'll be really good at it." A nice compliment, but little emotion in his voice or look. "Well, I have something lined up too. Just heard – got the job at a private golf course out in Ohio. Will be assisting the caddie master. I've always wanted to learn how to play golf, and this gives me the chance during my off hours."

Her look was not one of much enthusiasm either. *What does this have to do with picking a career choice?* she wondered.

Their last evening together was sober, subdued, perhaps even somber. A not so great take-out dinner eaten at Tyler's apartment, plus just a fair Italian red. Repeatedly, they stared into each other's eyes for long seconds at a time – an unbiased onlooker would immediately detect these two must be deeply in love. But no movement towards the bedroom, or even the couch. Just a long close hug, followed by a gentle kiss, and "take care of yourself, we'll stay in touch," although Tyler did sense a warm soft flow of tears as he hugged his cheek against hers. It was like that ancient expression *parting is such sweet sorrow.*

Tyler had one more goodbye to say. As usual, an evening knock on Professor Evans' apartment door would do it. But as Tyler approached the professor's apartment building, he clearly noticed the blinking red light reflecting off the sides of the building. It was from an ambulance. Then he saw two medically appareled men pushing a stretcher on wheels towards the vehicle. Ty quickly approached them. He noticed a sheet stretched out over what probably was a body. "Hey, what happened?" he eagerly asked.

"You can't ask us, fellow. This man is dead. We couldn't revive him. The security people are inside."

Tyler's first thought was dread, *but no, there are several people who occupy these* apartments. *It can't be...* Even so, he hustled inside and approached Professor Evans' apartment. The door was wide open, and he cautiously proceeded in. "Hey, this is sealed area. We're investigating..." a middle aged, uniformed campus security officer blurted out and then paused. "Look, any possible chance your name is Tyler, sophomore student?"

Tyler appeared stunned, and then quickly replied "Yes, that's me."

"Okay, son, sit down here. We need to talk. Looks like this Professor Evans who lived here just committed suicide. Probably sometime this afternoon he consumed two full bottles of very strong sleeping pills and put himself onto his bed, no covers on. He had left a note on the apartment manager's door to check his apartment around nine o'clock. He had left his door open a crack. On his chest he had an envelope, unsealed, with the words "For top prize sophomore student, Tyler." Of course, we opened it. That's you, right?"

Dumbfounded, Tyler looked up at the officer standing over him, and mumbled a weak "yes".

Pulling an envelope out of his pocket and reading from the single sheet of paper inside, the officer continued. "Ok, son, it reads:

*My dear scholarly friend Tyler,*

*Well lad, it looks like the end for me. I have no close family. I have been completely ostracized by my academic colleagues whom I had conversed with amicably for so many years at this once great university. My dissent is not permitted. Even though my parents and I were born here in America, they call me a White European to identify me. They always ask this question, but they don't get an answer – they don't know which sex I prefer. The English Literature classes I taught no longer have any meaning for me, and I am not serving my students well as I am forced to retire. I am too old and alone to try a venture off to your New America. I may as well learn if there really is another dimension out there somewhere which we humans cannot see or hear –we always called it 'heaven.' It always sounded so beautiful and peaceful. I can't wait to find out.*

*So, my astute young man, I leave it to you. You are so very intelligent, and I enjoyed immensely our many stimulating conversations. At least, until the last one, and I'm so sorry if I seemed depressed and short tempered with you. It was the beginning of the end for me. On the other hand, you are young, and you have choices. You can stay here, fight the uphill battle, and try to balance out this dreaded move to socialism, a movement always with great initial appeal but one that has never succeeded. Its ideals are noble but carrying it out is simply contrary to human nature. Or, you can join your close family in New America, be rewarded on your merits, and live happily ever after. The choice is yours. I pray for your success.*

*With great fondness,*
*your English Literature professor,*
*R.D. Evans PhD*

Tyler looked straight ahead, expressionless, not knowing what emotion he was feeling. His world had come crashing down.

# PART II

---- ★ ----

## NEW AMERICA

### 2033

# CHAPTER 18

★

## WHERE ARE WE

Alex was waiting for Papa Bear to finish his coffee before resuming their long conversation about cousin Tyler over in America and his losing his two great friends, John Frazier and Professor Evans. Unresolved yet in the story was what was happening in the topsy-turvy romance of Ty and his lovely Alyssa. In just one year they both had developed such strong opposing convictions. So, Alex reviewed some facts in his mind about just where he himself was now.

The huge landmass of Russia stretching from Eastern Europe all the way to the Pacific Ocean, about ten percent of the planet's land, is divided under the Russian central government into nine major administrative regions called 'krai's'. The Primorsky Krai borders Mongolian China to its West, North Korea to its South and the Sea of Japan to its East. It totals approximately 64,000 square miles of land, mostly forests and mountains. The largest city is Vladivostok, with some 500,000 population, a major military and shipping port for Russia. The city and both the highway and the railway going north then east into the vast Siberian landscape were excluded from the American lease deal. A wide assortment of ancient tribes inhabited the area prior to the Chinese Empire taking control. Anxious to rid any influence of the warlike, expansionist Mongolian Empire from influencing the budding nation of Russia, a deal was struck some

400 years ago for China to deed to Russia the huge Siberian landmass all the way to the Sea of Japan.

We think of Siberia as very remote and very cold, but this Krai a few years ago typically experienced average lows of minus five to plus nineteen highs in January and then a warm somewhat humid summer with an average low of sixty-three and average high of seventy-nine in August. Not so bad, New England like, but even better now that the planet's gradual warming period has lifted average temperatures even higher. The land area deeded to New America outside of Vladivostok and its corridor north contain a population just a little higher than that of the city. Those residents in the New America territory retained their Russian citizenship but voted overwhelmingly to enjoy a special citizenship status in New America. They all enjoyed plentiful work opportunities, excellent healthcare, and special schooling.

"Papa Bear!" Enough coffee, you will miss your nap this afternoon."

"Alex, my boy, I would rather chat with you than nap. Let's keep going," I responded quickly releasing my broadest smile. He may be old in years thought Alex, but he sure looked alert and peppy carrying on this conversation.

"Before you go on about Tyler, you know it's kind of depressing at the point where you paused for more coffee, so hey, let me tell you about my new friend Robert," said Alex. "I'm not sure if I want to hear any more about old America right now. It's so depressing. Don't they know from history that socialism and lack of order, and lack of moral standards, and lack of freedom never work?"

"Right, my boy, so let's talk about what we have here, here in new America. We can start with our government, our constitution, but okay you go first, tell me about your friend Robert."

"Yes, thanks," Papa Bear. "So, he's a great guy I met at university. We've really become good friends. He and his family just arrived three months ago. He said it's getting more and more difficult getting out of America. The government has learned they are losing too many of its best people and are trying to slow down the exodus to New America. Anyway, they got to Vladivostok by plane San Francisco to Tokyo to here. His dad is a skilled carpenter and landed a good job immediately. His mom and older sister also landed good jobs right away. He told me they all like to work and said the handouts in California were demeaning and making people lazy. He said there were drugs everywhere, crime was out of control, and that without police forces every company and every neighborhood and every school had to hire its own security force."

"Yes, yes, we know all that," I replied without a smile. "So, Robert."

Alex lit up. "Well, he loves it here already. He said here he is identified by his ability to work part time at something meaningful while trying to excel in his course work. Before over there he was identified as Black African American because his maternal grandmother was of African descent hundreds of years ago and his skin color was sort of light brown. They used to call them "colored people." You know, Papa Bear, none of that skin color stuff matters here. We are all assimilated New Americans identified by our merits."

"Right again, go on," I replied.

"Okay, so we are both taking a class on World History together, and it seems historical events are broken down as to which nation was warring or dominating at the time. Yes, the descriptions of religions and cultures come into play, but then there is always this violent explosion of one country or one culture seeking dominance over another. Robert and I have bonded and said we have to work hard to change that constant violence. I like the way he thinks. I guess the United Nations has done some good since there has not been a world war since 1945, but there sure have been lots of little ones..."

"So, where we are here, we have peace and prosperity here, right here in New America. That's not enough?" I interjected. "Son, have we escaped or are we still a part of world history?"

─── ★ ───

*From every mountainside, let freedom ring.*
Martin Luther King

# CHAPTER 19

★

# THE GOVERNMENT

"Let me explain, Alex. We here are an anomaly in the long fields of history. We have learned to get it right." I sat back and looked squarely into Alex's eyes to be sure he was listening. "Your world history – does it go back to the fact that we *homo sapiens,* we erect creatures with brains larger than the other mammals, go back a couple hundred thousand years? That our basic genes simply directed us to find mates, food sources, and shelters? That in that environment we could be competitive, even violent, when protecting those assets from marauders, and that we could also be compassionate, altruistic, and cooperative when it was to our advantage to do so? That after we learned how to cultivate crops and domesticate animals some ten thousand years ago, we became quote "civilized?" We developed languages and mathematics and tools and all kinds of civilized thoughts and things. But did you also learn that by early basic nature we could be inherently very disorderly? That over a period of only 3000 years in that long history, all the major religions were founded for the purpose of teaching rules of behavior and a hope for something better?" I paused. He was listening intently.

"No, Papa Bear," Alex responded to my questions. "We started with the Persian and the Egyptian Empires and the Babylonians not too long before Christ. Who was conquering who? Then the

Greeks and the Romans, but at least all those cultures developed great art and great architecture, and the Greek philosophers contributed wisdom lasting to this day."

"Good, great contributions besides developing weapons of war," I nodded.

Alex continued. "And all the empires – in the Americas – the Incas, the Aztecs, the Mayans, China and India in Asia. The spread of Islam from Spain to Indonesia, then the rise of Western Europe, the educated British developing great sailing vessels along with the Dutch, Portuguese and Spanish. All developing their cultures, expanding their empires, but the wars, Papa... why?"

"Because Alex as we sophisticated, we always wanted more. More possessions, more comforts, more power to control others to gain our own advantages. Sometimes, because each thought his own way superior to the others. Jihadist Islam, German Nazism. Marx's Communism. More wealth or greater expansion of ideology – you name it. If you don't give it to me, I'll take it by force."

"And now even more," Alex added. We are controlling electrons we cannot even see. Super computers in a tiny phone, the internet, GPS, electronic data manipulation."

"Right, Alex, so to control all that we have set up a government that first of all establishes the traditional role of preserving order and protection for its citizens. We establish basic rules and enforcement that one citizen cannot harm another – the right to life, and protection against outsiders who could do us harm. But beyond that our Constitution grants us fundamental freedoms, of speech, of movement, of gathering, of peaceful protests. We do not have a government run welfare state, but we do voluntarily have programs guaranteeing universal healthcare managed by private industry and old age programs to take care of the retired. We have a government that advises private industry and educational institutions on handling such ongoing issues as conflict management, learning, employee benefit programs, and good commercial practices. We don't have a government issuing mounds of regulations. We have ways to punish any selfish offenders."

"And am I right, Papa Bear, that there are term limits on government positions? We don't have a crazy system where a fortune and an undue amount of time are spent on running for reelection."

"Correct, one four year term for our representatives to the lower House, one eight year term for a senator, and one six year term for our president. And even better is our provision for a Balanced Budget except in times of a national emergency. Hey, as you know, even your Dad was elected a Representative some six years ago and he was so proud to serve as a Mediator on a dispute between upper management and a work crew over the number of hours of work a week issue where the jobs were physically demanding... Well, to sum it up, the old expression 'freedom is a blessing' young man, you have it here, and I know you will work hard to maintain it."

"So, how about all those other areas Dad keeps telling me about? How a typical government that sets up programs to help people, then over does it."

"Yes, Alex, he's right. Let's go back to our historic genes. Many times, and in many situations, an individual can't do enough alone. Both he and his community benefit, gain a better advantage, of cooperating and working together. We have learned through historical experience that individuals and companies can take selfish advantage, so we have anti-monopolistic laws, anti-trust laws, safety standards, building standards, food, and drug standards, and so on, but they each have limits. The enforcers stay within their bounds of competence. Very importantly our government has a very strong, well-funded, and competent Emergency Management Administration. Man caused and natural calamities often occur with little or no warning, and our new country is well prepared."

"Wow, neat," responded bright-eyed Alex. "I get it. Balanced. The right mix. Responsible freedom."

⎯⎯ ★ ⎯⎯

*Give me liberty or give me death*
Patrick Henry 1775

# CHAPTER 20

★

# FREE ENTERPRISE CAPITALISM

"Hope you don't mind," Alex chuckled, "but when I went out to the kitchen, I called Robert and he's going to stop over with some sandwiches. You know Papa Bear, we have been talking for hours, and you said you could skip your nap today. This had been so much fun to talk with you... although I'm not sure if I want you to continue the Tyler/Alyssa story. I just pray they will both show up here... But I want you to meet Robert."

"That would be fine Alex. You know the ladies. They can shop for hours on end, and then they meet friends and ..."

The apartment doorbell suddenly rang twice, interrupting Papa Bear's thoughts. Robert must be here already.

"Robert, meet my wise and quite young-at-heart great grand-father. We call him 'Papa Bear' and you can too." Alex smiled broadly and motioned Robert to shake hands.

"Happy to meet you, sir. Alex has told me so much about you."

"The pleasure is mine, Robert," I said. "Welcome. Sit down, please, sit here," I directed.

Alex broke in "Robert is taking a course in Economics and Free Enterprise, and Robert, Papa Bear was in the corporate business world for many years. I'm sure he has some words of wisdom."

"Long time ago, but tell me Robert, what types of things are you learning there in class?" I asked.

"Well, sir, for one we are studying all the different economic and political systems. The directed state sponsored and controlled semi-capitalist system of Communist China, the oligarchy system of Russia, the theocratic system of Iran, the socialistic system of some of the European countries and the Unites States, the capitalist system of some countries like Australia and New Zealand, the mixed systems of some countries, and the dictatorship systems of so many other countries. And, of course, we are learning that economic systems closely tie into the political systems of most countries. The two are bound together."

"Neat! And what is your take, Robert, on the merits and faults of these different political and economic systems, and can you compare them to what we have here?" I quizzed.

"Sure, now remember I haven't been here very long, and maybe I'm being taught a bias by the particular professor I have. My dad taught me that is always the case," Robert replied with a smile.

"Your dad is very wise," I noted. "Certainly, that's what happened in the America you came from, and to the extreme, huh?"

The two boys let out a short laugh before the conversation resumed. "Well, no question, in an oligarchy only a few really benefit, and if the goal is the best for the most, that's a huge weakness, and I'm told that's why the Russians welcome us here. Our royalties given them are spread around and help keep their system from crashing. Then the Chinese system, well that has benefited a third of their gigantic population, but you see giving some economic freedom without commensurate political freedom doesn't match. So, their secret police and military have to keep the lid on. Not much fun there, and it' an aging population because of their prior mandatory birth control measures.

"Now the so-called democratic socialist countries have homogeneous peoples who have accepted very high tax rates and stagnating economies – they do survive, but opportunity for the individual is limited. Upward mobility based on merit lags. America that I just left claims it's a democratic socialism, but with its wide mix of peoples all feuding for attention, its loss of its petroleum industry, its high crime and high drug use, its one party dominance – well as you both know, it's just a mess. So, I think I have to conclude that my new country here has learned from history what works and what doesn't work. Most people want to try something and succeed in life. We have the model for opportunity and rewards, right?"

"Think you nailed it, Robert," I said nodding my head in approval. "We have ample capital resources. We allow and encourage individuals and groups to start and build enterprises with minimum regulation and low tax rates. These enterprises succeed or fail or the merits of their leaders and workers and on market acceptance. The rewards are great for excellent performance. And compared to early capitalism, we truly have progressed in the best sense of that word. It is not politicians forcing the concept of progressive responsibility but the learning experience of two hundred years. We protect **all** our workers with fair pay for fair work, healthcare, unemployment and disability benefits, paid vacations, pensions, added education, and family leave. We have no need for unions. We avoid all that conflict. It is free enterprise at its best."

★

*Perfection is not attainable, but if we chase perfection
we catch excellence.*
Coach Vince Lombardi

# CHAPTER 21

★

## SOCIETY

All of a sudden, I realized it seemed to be getting quite late in the afternoon. But I did not feel the slightest bit fatigued. Forget my nap. The conversation with these two bright twenty year olds was so stimulating. They were so smart about all that was going on about themselves and their society. They were eager to learn, anxious to get out into the world and achieve, to succeed. I was delighted to press on. "So, you know where we are in this not so wonderful world of nations, and you know what kind of political and economic systems we have established here. Let's talk for a minute about the society we have created here. What strikes you the most?"

Both boys raised their chests, and both said virtually the same thing. "Freedom!" Alex almost shouted. "And every person has an opportunity to grow and succeed."

"Free to pursue my dreams," said Robert proudly.

"Okay, now does that freedom mean you can succeed or possibly fail or even land somewhere in between?" I countered.

"Yes," said Alex, "but in this land of equal opportunities not equal outcomes, we can, based on our own efforts and on our own merits, enjoy success or possibly suffer failure."

"But with failure," added Robert, "we learn, we pick ourselves back up, and try again. Isn't the striving a reward in itself?"

"A remarkable piece of wisdom," I noted. "Self-worth is a treasured virtue."

Alex changed the subject. "And we don't have or need drugs to feel a high. We have tons of entertainment, we drink the local beer, we play sports and games, and we dance with the coeds. We don't have legalized gambling – we like winning not based on luck, but effort. And if someone gets behind, mentally or physically, we have early detection systems and skilled assistance available immediately."

"Sounds good, Alex," added Robert. "And compared to where I just came from in old America with its tons of private security firms, I understand the police are well respected here. There is no brutality. Observance of the rules a civic responsibility, and if you don't like the rules, you have redress to try to change them."

"Yes, peaceful demonstrations a right, but violence is not condoned," said Alex. "These words I have read about – 'diversity and inclusion' – that's automatic here. We are all equal under the law. We all are of diverse whatever, but we all have an equal chance to do whatever we lawfully choose to do. We identify ourselves on merit, nothing else. With our own unique persons, yet we have assimilated into one American culture."

I sat back in my chair, smiling.

*It's not whether you get knocked down, it's whether you get up.*
Another Vince Lombardi

# CHAPTER 22

———— ★ ————

# THE LAND OF OPPORTUNITY

Darkness was approaching already in this early February month, and the two boys hugged me goodbye and said what a wonderful time they had sharing their thoughts with me. What a delightful day. They parted with me wishing them both much success in this land of great opportunity. The good wife had called and related that she got tied up with some old friends for the entire afternoon and told me to sit tight. She would bring home a delicious chicken dinner.

Alone with my thoughts now, I wondered how I would tell Alex about his cousin Tyler and his dear love Alyssa now midway through their junior years back in sad, sad old America. But I quickly shifted to the good things we are developing here in New America. Oh, to be twenty years old again. We have job and career opportunities so wide open, so diverse. The college educated have the sports and entertainment broadcasting and streaming services booming, computer expertise needed in so many fields, like the exciting use of artificial intelligence in the healthcare field, and add engineering, architecture, medicine. And then the many trade schools turning out more graduates each year as we are building so much infrastructure and housing in this growing population.

My mind shifted to the genius of our also leasing the Frontier Territory in the middle of Siberia from Russia. Some 700 years ago, much of the land had been conquered by the Mongolian Empire, the Russian's defense 400 years ago driving them back and eventually taking legal possession with a deal with China. Just fifty years ago this massive land mass was sparely populated. Thought to be cold and dark, it was perhaps best known for the many millions banished there by the czars and Stalin. The southern region was arid, the middle forest and the northern part under frozen top layers called the permafrost. While the winters were long and cold the summers were actually quite tolerable. Russia began a deliberate campaign to put more of its people into the southern portion and today millions live in a number of cities along the Trans-Siberian Railway. In the middle is Lake Baikal with the largest volume of lake water in the world. To the east side of the lake 400 miles is the city of Chita with a population of over 300,000. Yes, before the current warming period cold in winter with average high of only zero but conversely in July an average high of seventy-nine. Today's temperatures a few degrees higher. Just north of this somewhat arid but agriculturally rich grassland lies the central Siberian plateau with its frozen topsoil, the permafrost, but extremely rich in minerals. It is these minerals so valuable to the Americans and Europeans rapidly shifting away from oil, gas, and coal, believing they are thereby saving the planet, that are now being recovered by a combination of some melting of the permafrost and American engineering genius.

My last thoughts before I must have dozed off sitting back in my comfortable lounge chair were how the Americans back there had so messed up thinking that taking care of everyone's supposed needs by a supposed benevolent big government combined with a free-for-all in the streets would be the best for the most. It was a gross violation of human nature. Such an ideology had never worked before, and it failed again except for the few rich and powerful elites. If people have to strive to survive and prosper, they will do it. If there is an easy way out, they will take it. Then here in forging this New America, with our balanced working combination of both our competitive and altruistic traits, we have created such a perfect little new country. But what is the future for the rest of humanity?

--- ★ ---

*Grow or die.*
The Storyteller

# PART III

★

## AMERICA
## SOMEWHERE

# CHAPTER 23

★

## A HOPE AND A PRAYER

"Hey everyone! His eyes are open. He's awake!" I heard someone screaming. "Papa Bear, it's me, Tyler. Can you hear me?"

"Yes, yes, I hear you. Don't scream." I looked around, not sure where I was at first. I surely recognized my great grandson Tyler, and there was my other great grandson Alex, and approaching me was Ty's girlfriend Alyssa. I quickly realized I was lying down in a bed in a room I didn't recognize, maybe in a hospital. I saw a nurse also approaching. She smiled and said she would go out and call the doctor. "Where am I?" I asked the three youngsters. The room was bright but looked somewhat sterile. Yes, I must be in a hospital. I was now looking into the bright faces of three smiling ... teenagers? Then I felt the uncomfortable intravenous feed into my arm. *What happened to me?*

"Papa Bear, you have been in a coma for two weeks. They don't know what happened to you. Your vital signs are all good. No fall, no stroke, we don't know..."

"Two weeks?" I muttered. "What day is it? No, what year is it?"

Alex instantly answered. "Papa Bear, it's November first, 2030. You will be so happy. You will be able to vote for our president next week."

"2030?" I replied quizzing my mind. "It's not 2033? Wait, how old are you three? Are you in school?"

"Geez," said Alex. "Your mind was so perfect, Papa Bear. Must be you were asleep so long. We are all 18, seniors in high school. We came to visit you on Saturday, today, when we're not in school. Mom, dad, your kids come during the week. I'll call them right now and tell them the good news."

"So, I've been dreaming? Part nightmare, part ecstasy? Listen, have you ever heard of New America? It's in Siberia, Russia."

The three teenagers all broke into laughter at the same time. "Siberia. That's crazy. You **have** been dreaming," said Alex still smiling broadly.

I stared into the bright, obviously happy faces of these three beautiful kids. Both boys so handsome and this girl absolutely radiant. "Yeah, maybe. Maybe I had a long dream. Seemed so real. Tell me. Seniors in high school, right? Anybody have a course in Economics, Political Science, Sociology?"

The three couldn't wait to reply. "I take a Political Science class and love it," said Alex without pause.

"I have a Social Studies class and I'm going to major in Sociology when I go to college," said Alyssa.

"We don't have Economics per say, but I discuss it a lot with my dad, and I think I'll go to Business School next year and major in it," said Tyler.

"Fine, fine," I continued. "So, do we have only one political party now in America? Do we have socialism? Is capitalism dead? Do we have a free press? Free speech? Is dissent allowed? Are the police forces disbanded? Do we have high crime in the streets and legal drugs everywhere?" I wanted to go on, but the three simultaneously broke out in loud laughter.

"Papa Bear! Where have you been?" Alex said with a broad grin. "Don't you remember ten years ago when all that nonsense was thrown out and the American people reestablished all our basic principles. The American Dream is alive. The two major parties go back and forth in majorities, open to working together, compromising on complex issues at both ends of the political spectrum. They put their foot down on violent protests. They have kept taxes reasonably low. They try to balance their budgets. They have increased government aid to the needy, to the poor minority neighborhoods. Legal and political equality now for everyone. "Out of many, one", meaning out of many diverse backgrounds we assimilate into one American society. Educational grants for all ages and trade school training have increased tremendously. They have created a fairly efficient universal health care system with little government involvement other than for the aged and the poor. No, both ardent conservatives and the left progressive liberals don't get everything they clamor for, but that middle ground is holding. It's like my history class I remember – the sage old Benjamin Franklin at the long debating sessions at the 1787 Convention to develop a United States Constitution and his shouting out 'Compromise, compromise'! Papa Bear! We've done that, and the American Dream for all is alive and well. We are truly exceptional in this world."

I stared at Alex in awe. I was temporarily speechless... "And China has not overrun us?" I asked meekly.

"Ha!" shouted Tyler. "Not a chance. We have slowed down our fast jump to a so-called Green Economy. Reason prevails. World temperatures in this warming period have risen very, very modestly so we are developing new technologies as the market allows which means the American economy is very strong while the Chinese economy has slowed with their aging population and their tons of political dissent.

I must have still had a look of incredulity on my face. "And our military? The world's conflicts?"

Alex with his Political Science grounding spoke up. "We have a strong military with listening post bases around the world to be alert to any threats to us, but we have no troops fighting anywhere. Sure, the conflicts continue, especially in Africa and the Middle East. Will they ever get settled? It will take some great leaders of the big nations to finally resolve ongoing natural conflict without resorting to violent behaviors."

This all was so hard for me to believe. My hope has been sustained and my prayers answered. My long wild dream is over. America is America. Then I heard and saw the nurse talking to someone who must be my doctor in the doorway. The young ones all moved towards them. I closed my eyes for a moment. I thought to myself – *Is this all just another dream?*

*Men at some time are masters of their fates*
Shakespeare

CPSIA information can be obtained
at www.ICGtesting.com
Printed in the USA
FSHW021000231121
86287FS